David Zoppetti

ICHIGENSAN
— THE NEWCOMER —

Translated from the Japanese by Takuma Sminkey

Ichigensan – The Newcomer

by David Zoppetti
translated by Takuma Sminkey

Published by Ōzaru Books, an imprint of BJ Translations Ltd
Street Acre, St Nicholas-at-Wade, BIRCHINGTON, CT7 0NG, U.K.
https://ozaru.net/ozarubooks

First edition published 1 March 2011 (minor revisions made in 2023)
ISBN: 978-0-9559219-4-0

Also available on Kindle, and in German translation as "*Ichigensan — Der Neuankömmling*".

CHAPTER ONE

I first met Kyōko during my junior year as a university student. A heavy sleet was falling during that early afternoon in late January, and I was suffering from a terrible hangover.

On the edge of campus, there was a compact red brick building with a small lounge for foreign students in the corner of the ground floor. Because the room protruded out from the building like a peninsula and students from various countries always gathered there, everyone called the room *Dejima*, in reference to the artificial island in Nagasaki Harbor constructed for foreign traders in the seventeenth century.

We hung out in *Dejima* whenever we had a free moment. In winter, gentle warmth emanating from the small kerosene heater reminded us of our home countries, and there was always a full pot of good coffee available. In summer, the antique air conditioner we all chipped in for rattled ominously, and in spring and fall, a refreshing breeze gently streamed in through the open windows, carrying the sounds of campus life. It was a comfortable little room, with a distinct touch for each season.

On that particular day, the sleet had been falling steadily since morning. A downpour of such intensity made you wonder what type of cloud could possibly contain so much of the stuff.

When I entered *Dejima*, several Chinese students were watching an afternoon entertainment show on the old TV donated by former foreign students. I tossed off my wet leather jacket and headed straight to the sofa at the far end of the room. I stretched out on my back and closed my eyes. The sleet on my face turned into cool droplets and dribbled pleasantly through my hair. That was the last sensation I was aware of before drifting off into a deep sleep.

The night before, on the way home from my part-time job, I had spent some time browsing through the secondhand bookstores of Umeda in Ōsaka, and had purchased a first edition of Tanizaki Jun'ichirō's *Kagi* (The Key)—without even looking at the price. I must admit to an incurable weakness for old books. I had then returned to my room with the firm intention of reading late into the night. I sat down at the *kotatsu*, a low table with a heating device underneath and a quilt to cover one's legs, lit my pipe, and placed a bottle of whisky within reach.

The smell of the tobacco had gradually pervaded the room. The burning sensation of alcohol slid to my stomach like white lead, yet left a faint sweet aftertaste on my tongue. The coarse texture of the pages under my fingertips conveyed a strong sense of authenticity. Utterly at ease with all these sensations, I had lost myself in the sexual world of the elderly couple Tanizaki was depicting. Intrigued by how expressions of love and desire can transcend age, I had persevered late into the night. But apparently stupor and drowsiness overcame me, for when I woke up, the world had well moved into another day.

How long had I slept on the sofa? When I came to my senses, a woman's distant voice drifted into my dim consciousness.

"So it would be a tremendous help if a foreign student could read to her. We live alone, so we aren't able to pay much, but I'm sure it would be a learning experience for both, and also a chance to make a new friend."

She spoke in an even tone of voice, but rather low for a woman. I opened my eyes halfway and rolled over slightly towards the speaker. My head was throbbing. A young woman was sitting beside her. As both were facing Nakayama-*san*, a female member of the office staff, I couldn't see their faces, but I was sure they were mother and daughter. One of these intuitions that can't be explained by logic or reason, but nonetheless grasps you as an indubitable certainty.

I tried to bring my mind back to the reality of *Dejima* but wasn't able to shake off the feeling of persistent drowsiness. The mother was about forty years old. Her black hair, which was twisted back into a smooth knot, had a few gray strands, but rather than hinting to the beginning of aging, they gave the impression of having naturally settled there a long time ago. As my gaze moved down, something about the shape of her neck brought to mind the old-fashioned Japanese women from the world of Tanizaki, the sensual universe I had been immersed in until late last night. Perhaps the impression was enhanced by the fact that she was wearing a kimono.

The young daughter had her hair tied back into a ponytail with a purple hair band. Staring at the ground, she remained perfectly still and quiet. She wore jeans and a gray sweater that seemed soft to the touch.

Unaccountably intrigued, I tried to pick up the flow of the conversation. But there wasn't any. They were finished speaking. The two women stood up almost simultaneously and bowed slightly to Nakayama-*san*. "So if you find someone, please let us know. We'll be waiting for your call." After the mother said this in a clear voice, the two headed towards the door.

Then something curious happened. Something so trivial I would have missed it if I hadn't been paying attention. But it caught my eye as a message addressed directly to me. As both women were walking the short distance from Nakayama-*san*'s desk to the door, the daughter gently pressed against her mother's arm and clumsily brushed against the stove, the bookcase, and some chairs along the way.

Battling my horrendous hangover, I sat up and took my time surveying the room. The other students showed no signs of having noticed the two women. The Chinese students, still absorbed in their TV program, were laughing uproariously. Sometimes they made comments in Chinese about the jokes and laughed even more. The Japanese student who had been reading the *Japan Times* while munching on a ham sandwich kept chomping away with unabated enthusiasm. His brows were furrowed in total concentration on the article. Even Nakayama-*san*, who had attended on the two women with her usual cheerfulness, was sorting papers—as if nothing had happened.

When I stood up, my head reeled and the room tilted as if I were standing on the deck of the sinking Titanic. After closing and re-opening my eyes, I was relieved to discover that *Dejima* had returned to its original horizontal position.

I looked out the window and caught a glimpse of the pair as they disappeared behind the adjacent brick building. The daughter, pressed up close to her mother, who was holding up a Japanese-style umbrella, walked falteringly. After they disappeared, I watched the sleet fall silently on the campus.

Having served myself a cup of hot coffee, I headed over to Nakayama-*san*'s desk with unsteady steps. I sat down in one of the chairs vacated by the women and took a whiff of the vapor rising from my cup. Nothing like the tantalizing aroma of a good cup of coffee to give you the confidence to face any problem in the world.

"Who were those women?" I asked, after taking a sip of coffee, my words a bit slurred.

Nakayama-*san* lifted her eyes from the papers, which appeared to be student entrance exam applications, and looked at me.

"Well, well. You certainly look awful; another rough night?"

Before I could reply, she went on without pausing for breath.

"About those ladies? Well I received a call the other day. The thing is, the daughter's blind. I don't know all the details, but it seems she went to a school for the blind in Tōkyō, and last year, graduated from a regular college. She has just moved to Kyōto with her mother, and since she's not planning on working, she's looking for someone to do face-to-face reading once in a while."

"Face-to-face reading?"

"Yeah, I never heard of it either, but I guess it means reading books out loud to her."

As she spoke, she began stuffing envelopes.

"Anyway, her mother found out that foreign students here are involved in cultural exchanges and volunteer work and talked it over with her daughter. They decided that a foreign student would be okay, even if he makes a few mistakes or has an accent. She said her daughter hadn't had much contact with foreigners. And today, they came by to introduce themselves."

Sipping my coffee, I listened to Nakayama-*san*'s explanation.

So she was blind. No wonder she walked that way. Through the cloud rising from my cup, I stared at the sleet falling on the campus. I had sobered up, and my head was surprisingly clear.

There were a million things I suddenly wanted to do in life. To start with, I desperately wanted to meet that young woman.

That day, I decided to head straight back home. Even if I had remained at university, I was in no frame of mind to concentrate on classes. The sleet continued until dark. On a day like that, there was nothing to do but read. Just as there are days when there's nothing to do but have a barbecue by the river, there are days whose significance is forever lost if they are not spent indulged in intense reading. I settled down in my small room and turned on the kerosene stove. Slowly recovering from my hangover, I picked up Tanizaki's novel.

It was nice to relax in this room that had been so difficult to find because of the various obstacles I had to overcome. To begin with, I didn't go to the university's housing office until the middle of March, a couple of weeks before the beginning of classes, so there were hardly any rooms available. But that wasn't all. I had arrived from overseas with… a rabbit. As a consequence, even if there was a room available, once landlords found out that their potential tenant was a foreign student with a rabbit, they usually refused outright for some futile reason. I was a Johnny-come-lately, with a living ball of fur to make matters worse.

I had been homeless up until three days before my first classes. So when I finally did find a lodging I was truly relieved. But this didn't last long. The place was rundown beyond imagination. The traditional Kyōto-style house probably hadn't been renovated once since its construction over three hundred years ago, and I had to pay 25,000 yen a month—which was outrageous by Kyōto standards—for the second-floor room I rented. Looking back, I think it was a total rip-off.

At any rate, I shared a kitchen and toilet with five or six other students, and since there weren't any rooms with a tub or shower, I went to a small *sentō* public bathhouse about fifty meters down the street, called the *Tsuru no Yu* (Crane Baths). The kitchen and the narrow Japanese-style toilet with a broken lock were both located in the building's courtyard, which means outside, and using either of them during the winter months required a considerable degree of courage and determination.

Those shared facilities were shockingly filthy. In the kitchen, there was always a stack of dirty dishes infested with maggots. Floating in the stagnant brown water of the cups were cigarette butts, abandoned there forever. The drain of the sink was coated with mold. It was a kitchen that would even make a cockroach seriously contemplate suicide. The raw garbage scattered all around the house provided welcome free food for brazen stray cats, and every night they came yowling, "Hey, as always, thanks for the treat." I often heard the sounds of lightning-speed fights over unidentifiable leftovers. In front of everyone's room were piles of textbooks, comic books, copies of *Playboy* and other magazines. Wondrous structures, always on the verge of collapse.

The toilet was beyond description. Back when I was in the army, I had gone through a horrible experience at a small training outpost in the mountains. Whenever someone entered the latrine, shared by a hundred huge fellows, his eyes immediately began to burn from the stench. Even the toughest guys became dizzy and nauseated. It was a latrine version of Hell. But the toilet at the boardinghouse was so bad that I almost felt nostalgic for the questionable sanitary cleanliness of that army outpost.

Our landlord was a small, pleasant man who ran a butcher shop nearby. Every day, he would come to the house, and driven to despair by the chaos, would plaster the walls with notices entreating us to clean up after ourselves. The signs listed complicated rules written in old-fashioned Japanese. The students ignored them completely and went on messing up the place with an indifference bordering on cruelty.

Nevertheless, I soon developed an unaccountable fondness for this old house, which on the surface seemed so discomforting. Probably because my own room was so cozy. I don't know much about traditional Japanese architecture, but next to the *tokonoma* alcove in this six-mat room were staggered shelves, with beautifully curved protrusions along the front edges. The top shelf was lined with gold-colored paper.

A small river, the Shirakawa, flowed behind the house and I could hear its pleasant gurgling from my room. On my way back from the public bath, I liked to stand on the nearby stone bridge, drinking beer from a can and listening to the song of the flowing water. Weeping willows lined both banks of the river, and ducks would paddle quietly beneath their drooping branches. Gazing at the scene always brought me a feeling of deep tranquility. Those ducks swimming in complete silence at dusk created a little world that neared perfection.

The week following the day of sleet flew by in no time. The month of January, exhaling white breath, moved with gentle steps to February. The cold days continued, but the sky was blissfully clear. Every day I attended classes, and every day I went to my part-time job.

I met Kyōko on Saturday. Nakayama-*san* called from *Dejima* to introduce me and then explained how to get there. According to the map she drew for me, the house was behind Kyōto University near the Yoshida-jinja shrine, located on a small hill. Before leaving my dwelling, I spread a map out on my desk and confirmed the location by juxtaposing the one Nakayama-*san* had drawn for me. Kurodani, the name of the area, was indeed written there in small characters.

When I stepped outside, it was still bitter cold. But Kyōto was covered by a cloudless winter sky, and the morning air was invigorating. I hopped on my scooter and headed north up the Shirakawa-dōri street. On my right, running parallel to the street, rose the Higashiyama mountains, crystal clear against the blue sky.

I stopped in front of an old-fashioned wooden gate with a thatched roof. It looked more like the entrance to a hermitage or a small shrine than one to someone's home. There was neither a nameplate nor a mailbox. Slightly concerned, I checked the map, but I was in the right place.

When I hesitantly passed through the small gate, it felt as if I had stepped into a fairy tale. Surrounded by earthen walls, were four or five snug looking houses, with a narrow gravel path threading its way among them. The small gardens between the houses were strewn with stones, moss, and an innumerable number of small bonsai-like plants. Although cut off from the outside world by high walls, the grounds were surprisingly sunny. Everything was so quiet one could almost hear the hushed breathing of the surrounding plants.

"Are you looking for something?"

Distracted by the miniature world before my eyes, I hadn't noticed the woman with a broom in her hands standing by the entrance of the first house. Her flustered tone of voice was horrendously out of harmony with the peaceful surroundings.

"Oh, I'm sorry. Is the Nakamura residence near here?" I asked hastily.

The broom lady propped her instrument against the door, traipsed over to me as if it were a total bother, and pointed to the house at the far end of the garden.

"If you're looking for the Nakamuras, they live over there."

I thanked her and passed beneath the passageway that connected a house on my left to its annex on my right. Sensing the woman's eyes upon me, I headed down the narrow gravel path. It was such an intense stare, I feared ending up with a hole burned in my back.

When I reached the house, I was at a loss again.

There was a nameplate that read:

The
Nakamuras
Yuriko
Kyōko

But there was no bell or knocker.

"Excuse me!" I yelled, my voice echoing in a futile way, as if I were calling from the rim of the Grand Canyon. Nonetheless, the front door soon opened, and I was greeted by the smiling face of Nakamura-*san*, whom I had only seen from behind at *Dejima*. Meeting her for the first time, I was struck by her familiar and amiable manner.

"Well, hello! So you managed to find us. Please come in," she said, holding the door for me.

The inside of the house looked like a natural extension of the gardens outside. Leading from the entrance was a narrow hallway with small *tatami* rooms on either side. The many pieces of furniture, vases, and other small objects, were all neat and tidy. I wondered how a blind person could live with so many things bound to get in the way. But then again, what I considered as obstacles might serve as signposts for her.

We passed through the winding corridor, went up a flight of steps and reached the innermost room, which was the living room. To the right was a large sliding-glass window that overlooked the garden I had just passed through. I could see a narrow veranda outside. Kyōko was kneeling at a *kotatsu* in front of the window. From behind her, the faint winter sunlight streamed into the room.

Something about Kyōko's appearance moved me. She had a book in front of her, and her hands were moving across the page, which was strewn with innumerable dots. She followed the complicated patterns with her fingertips. Although the scene was new for me, I immediately knew that she was reading Braille.

With her eyes almost closed and the tips of her slender fingers softly caressing the surface of the page, Kyōko looked completely at ease. She had full lips and a straight nose. Her eyebrows traced two delicately balanced arcs. I thought she was very attractive.

She undoubtedly sensed us standing there at the threshold, but she showed no sign of raising her head, apparently intending to continue reading until reaching a good place to stop.

Silence prevailed a little more until Kyōko's fingers moved away from the lines of raised dots. Nakamura-*san*, as if she had been waiting for that precise moment, was the first to break the silence.

"Kyōko, our guest arrived," she said, gesturing for me to sit down at the *kotatsu*.

"This is my daughter, Kyōko."

Kyōko raised her head in my direction and said, "Hello."

"Hello," I returned her greeting and gave my name.

Kyōko seemed to be determining my position and the height of my head. I was a bit surprised as I watched her face from up close. When she occasionally lifted her long-lashed eyelids, I could catch a glimpse of her eyes. They were perfectly normal. It sounds silly, but I hadn't imagined them like this. They were neither all white, nor were the pupils strangely dilated. If I had to guess, I would say they weren't quite focused, but one wouldn't notice without paying close attention.

It was the first time I met a blind person, and I could hardly believe that such normal-looking eyes could not see.

I sat down at the *kotatsu* across from Kyōko, urged on by Nakamura-*san*.

"I'll make some tea," she said, as she discreetly left the room.

For a while, we sat in silence. Kyōko closed her Braille book and idly traced the edge with her fingers.

"This is a nice room," I said. When I'm with someone, I tend to get nervous when there's no conversation for too long.

"Please put yourself at ease," Kyōko said, not responding to my comment.

This came as a total surprise. She had been sitting in the formal *seiza* posture, with both legs folded under her. I had felt compelled to join her, but to tell the truth, as I had always had a hard time sitting like that, I was praying for her mother to hurry back, notice my agony, and relieve me by saying the words of grace—"Put yourself at ease"—which Kyōko had just expressed.

But Kyōko couldn't possibly know how I was sitting.

"Hey, how did you figure that out?" I blurted out, as I adjusted the position of my legs.

"I've been blind since birth, so I notice all kinds of things without seeing them," she nonchalantly explained. "Sounds that people don't pay attention to. Hints of movement. The smell of things. Subtle shifts in the air. These things give me a fair idea of what's going on around me."

The explanation was convincing.

"Well, that makes sense," I said. I didn't know if all blind people had such close to supernatural powers, but crossing my legs in a more comfortable position, I thanked her in my heart.

Again, there was a short silence.

"You don't have a Kansai accent at all," I said, not being able to come up with anything better. Silence makes me edgy, but I'm no good at small talk either.

"I guess you're right. I've spent most of my life in Tōkyō. I was born there, and that's where I went to school." She finally stopped fiddling with her book, and after reaching to check the location of the *kotatsu* tabletop, she placed her hands on top of it.

"My father was originally from Kyōto. He died in a car accident when I was small, though… Anyway, we've got a lot of relatives here in Kyōto we used to visit a lot. But these visits were always short, and when we returned to Tōkyō, I quickly went back to speaking standard Japanese. So I guess I never picked up much of the Kansai dialect."

When she spoke, she always kept her face turned in my direction. Seeing her *look* at me in such a way made it increasingly difficult to believe that she was really blind.

Her mother returned.

We drank our tea and continued with small talk. After a while, I started to wonder about the primary purpose of my visit and asked, "About this face-to-face reading, how were you considering doing it?"

Kyōko checked the position of her saucer with her left hand and placed her teacup on top of it. There was a little clinking sound of porcelain against wood. She turned to face me again.

"You know, I just love literature. Both Japanese and foreign. But in Japan, there's not much available in Braille. Just a few representative works by a few famous authors. There's an obnoxious number of books on acupuncture, moxibustion, massage, and other healing methods. Then there's the Bible and a ridiculous number of books on Christianity. Even the 6 volumes of the law codes have been put into Braille. But honestly, how many people could possibly want to read that stuff? This kind of thing really exasperates me. Why do we have to read books so boring that other people hardly look at just because we're blind?" She was rather worked up.

I realized she had a point, but I didn't know what to say.

"When I was in Tōkyō and wanted to read more literature, I had people from the blind school or volunteers from the Braille transcription group read to me. Or I bought recordings of books on tape. When we moved here, I wanted to continue something similar. That's when I heard about the foreign students at your university and decided to ask for some help."

Listening to Kyōko's confession about literature, I was somewhat moved. Because I myself happened to be majoring in Japanese literature.

Initially, there was no particular reason for my coming to Japan. I've always enjoyed traveling, and after turning twenty, I had spent a long time living a *nomadic* lifestyle. For nearly five years, I had traveled to various places, lived in various settings, and met numerous people.

Eventually, I came to the realization that moving around like a Bohemian was in my nature, perhaps even my mission in life. At any rate, I had basically wandered to Japan on nothing more than a vague, nomadic impulse.

Most people, however, didn't accept such a vague explanation. They would stare at me as if to say, "Surely, you've got a more specific and sensible reason than that!" They obviously wanted to hear a more convincing story. "You followed a woman here, didn't you?" they would say. Or "You were drawn to the mysterious world of the Orient, weren't you?" But I couldn't come up with a tale to satisfy them, for indeed only a vague, *nomadic impulse* had brought me to Japan.

My choice to major in Japanese literature originated in a similar way. Generally speaking, a major in literature isn't going to lead you to very exciting places: it hardly provides any prospect for steady employment, and has no practical applications. Speaking with other foreign students, I found out that they were attracted to Japan as an economic power and were doing research to discover the secret of Japan's economic growth. They had a very clear goal in mind: to use knowledge acquired in Japan in order to better their home countries.

I might deserve some respect if I had chosen Japanese literature out of a desire of learning. But unfortunately, that wasn't the case. I didn't have any academic motives. I didn't wish to learn about Japan's various customs and lifestyles through literature, nor did I intend to return to my country to teach all of this someday. Japanese literature was just another vague impulse, which seen from the Ministry of Education's point of view, meant I was surely walking on dangerously thin ice as far as my status as an "international student" was concerned.

What saved me was my passion for reading. I mean *pure* love of reading. Just as some people have a genuine love of eating Hobson's strawberry ice cream with coconut powder topping, I had a pure love of reading. Ever since I was a child, I did nothing but read. I read whatever I could get my hands on, one book after another. No matter how much I read, I was always hungry for more. I also read tremendously while I was working on a ship. Once my tasks were completed, I had all the free time in the world. In that sense, a long voyage at sea is ideal for losing one's self in literature.

This excessive consumption of books, however, didn't mean I had learned much. The moment I finished reading something, all the specifics vanished from my memory, leaving behind only vague emotions. So when I entered university, I couldn't quote passages from famous works. I was also awful at conveying my impressions in specific words.

Come to think of it, I perhaps had one more reason for choosing to major in literature. I was fascinated by used books—not only in Japan but also throughout the world. I had no sense for money and was constantly plagued by poverty. Even so, as soon as my livelihood was settled in a country, I'd start accumulating used books as if it were going out of style. And when I set out on my travels again, I blithely sold them off—without any melancholy or regrets. I had what you might call an abnormally strong desire to own old books for a short period of time.

After settling down in Kyōto, I entered every used bookstore I could find and purchased all kinds of expensive first editions and reprints. When I got paid for my part-time job, I often took the slow night train to Tōkyō. The next day was spent browsing endlessly through the used bookstores lining the streets of the Jinbō-chō district. Standing between the high shelves, I picked out such precious and rare books as Natsume Sōseki's *Kokoro* (The Heart of Things) in a beautiful case, Futabatei Shimei's *Ukigumo* (The Drifting Clouds) illustrated with satirical prints, or a copy of Tanizaki's *Irezumi* (The Tattooer) with a worn binding. After agonizing over what to do, I hurriedly put them back where I had found them.

But then in the end, I always bought books that were far beyond my economic means and without any practical value. Then I'd take the slow night train back to Kyōto, thrilled about my new acquisitions, but also anguished by an overwhelming sense of impending bankruptcy.

Steevie just loved gnawing on those old books.

Unlike cats and dogs, rabbits don't make any specific sounds and are known as little more than cute animals. I can assert that this is a totally unfair and prejudicial view. If you live with a rabbit for a few years, you'll realize it has a strong personality, which doesn't prevent it from being surprisingly sociable. Steevie was both smart and stubborn; when it came time to make a point, he acted as if he were the lord of all creation—probably because of his foreign origin.

Steevie's residence was a gray plastic box. Attached to the metal mesh door were two little white containers, one for food, and the other for water. The bottom of the box had a wooden lattice covered with straw, so he wouldn't walk in his excrement. I cleaned the box and changed the straw once every three days. I performed these chores conscientiously wherever I was, even when traveling or working on a ship. I firmly believe in investing time and affection in a relationship whether dealing with a ravishing woman or a twenty-centimeter long rabbit. You wouldn't find a rabbit owner as dedicated as me, even if you were to search the entire world.

Rabbits don't read and usually don't write. They don't give a fiddler's fart about exchange rate fluctuations, the weather, world affairs, or basically anything. They're a carefree lot. Apart from scrupulously cleaning themselves and sleeping, there's not much going on. But when it comes to meals! They simply have an insatiable appetite. The two containers were emptied—at an unbelievable speed—several times a day. Steevie was not the type to pass time patiently until his next feeding—he had issues with waiting as well as his weight. Whenever his rabbit food or water ran out, he put his front feet into the containers, latched onto the door with his front teeth, and rattled the box with incredible force. That was something of a racket. Steevie knew perfectly well how effective this stupendous commotion was. Whether writing a report, drinking with friends, or *cultivating international relations* with some cute co-ed, I would immediately cease everything to provide fresh food and water.

Rabbits are gnawers, like the active beavers that build dams in the rivers of Canada. This means that if they don't gnaw on something hard regularly, their front teeth grow longer and longer.

Steevie was no exception. If he didn't get his jaws biting into something solid for a while, his teeth would start stretching out like a mammoth's tusks. If that happened, I had no choice but to take him to the vet and have his teeth cut. Needless to say, Steevie detested such barbaric procedures. To prevent excessive growth of his teeth, Steevie went on crunching wallpaper, posts, telephone cords, *tatami* mats—and of course, used books—whenever he had the opportunity. As I always let him roam free when I was home, he had plenty of chances to get into mischief. And no matter how close an eye I kept on him, he always managed to destroy something.

Thanks to Steevie, my damage security deposit had never been refunded. Anyway, I had figured that this amounted to what I would have to pay for a vet to cut and polish his teeth, and had basically given up trying to keep things under control.

I began visiting Kyōko about once or twice a week. Most of the time, I went to see her when my classes were finished, but I also occasionally visited on weekends.

It was springtime on campus. The cheerleading club gathered daily during the noon recess, and with a frenzy that made you wonder if they hadn't suffered some kind of brain damage, they waved their arms and screamed at the top of their lungs. Co-eds would gather in front of the bulletin board announcing the nearly daily canceling of classes, and rejoice or grieve according to which fate awaited them. A university campus is a theater stage where innumerable little dramas unfold.

After classes, I hopped on my scooter and headed south down the gentle incline of the Shirakawa-dōri street. Each time I walked through the small gate with the thatched roof and entered the mysterious garden, I was struck by the same peculiar sensation I had experienced the first time. Everything was so perfectly quiet, so remote from the reality of my everyday surroundings. When I reached the house, Kyōko's mother was always waiting for me at the entrance. For no special reason, seeing her standing there, not uttering a word, just smiling at me, always made my heart start to race. But she never showed any sign of noticing. She simply bowed slightly and led me to the warm living room at the rear of the small house.

That was where Kyōko sat. Usually, she would be at the *kotatsu* moving her fingertips across intricate little groupings of raised dots. Occasionally, with her head turned slightly away from the television set, she would be giggling as she *listened* to a show.

After Kyōko's mother brought us tea or coffee, we were left alone. At such moments, I was always moved by her distinct beauty. When I laid the two or three books that I had under my arm on the *kotatsu*, Kyōko would notice the sound, slowly turn her head in my direction, and ask, "What did you bring today?" in lieu of a greeting.

The first book I read to her was a modern version of Mori Ōgai's *Maihime* (The Dancing Girl), which I happened to be studying for my courses. Even with a modern adaptation, my reading at the time was as faltering as a toddler's first steps. Struggling to follow the complex flow of words, my voice had no spark to it whatsoever. And whenever I hit a passage where I had to read one unknown *kanji* after another, I became totally flustered.

One Saturday afternoon in late February, I was putting on another one of my unimpressive reading performances; it was so slow that I began to feel sorry for Kyōko, who was quietly listening to me. But I tried to convince myself that this was basically volunteer work, and that I therefore didn't have to put up with any complaints.

I lifted my head from the text, which looked like an agitated sea, and glanced over at her. She didn't seem particularly dissatisfied. Using an alcove pillar as a backrest, she sat facing the window, with her legs hugged to her chest and her chin resting on her knees. She appeared calm, but at the same time, I sensed in her something extremely fine and vulnerable. Before I could grasp what it was—it had filled the room like the faint fragrance of plum blossoms.

Perhaps because I had stopped reading, or else because she sensed I was staring at her, she looked somewhat embarrassed and whispered, "What is it? Why did you stop? Please carry on."

But I didn't continue right away.

"This garden has quite a variety of beautiful plants. Who takes care of it?"

"Sometimes my mother does," answered Kyōko, as she traced the lines of her lips with her fingers, "but usually it's the lady who lives in the house near the entrance."

This brought back to memory the broom lady I had bumped into on my first visit. Somehow I couldn't picture her meticulously tending the delicate plants in this garden. Another short silence fell over the room. I filled it with a sigh that had no particular meaning and resumed reading.

As usual, after reading for about an hour, my concentration was scattered like autumn leaves blown by the wind, and my voice had become dreadfully hoarse.

"Why don't we stop here for today?" said Kyōko.

My head was reeling, and my lips and jaws had become as stiff as old chewing-gum, so I was greatly relieved. I slowly closed the book and put it back on the *kotatsu*. When I looked outside, it was dark and the small garden was barely visible. As darkness grew deeper, the large sliding glass door facing the garden gradually turned into a mirror, and the reflection of the two of us sitting there became more and more distinct. It was like being in an old movie theater, where the lights are slowly dimmed and the first scenes of an impressionist movie appear on the screen.

Kyōko reached for her pack of cigarettes and pulled one out. She checked the position of the lighter flint with her finger, flicked the lighter until it lit, and then held the flame to the tip of her cigarette. However, as she was holding it pointing slightly downward instead of horizontally, one entire side of the cigarette caught fire with a crackle. Kyōko got flustered and dropped the cigarette on the tabletop of the *kotatsu*. The flame went out instantly, but the room smelt of smoke pretty bad.

She sighed.

"I just can't get this done properly. My mother's always telling me to quit, but every now and then, I just feel like a smoke."

"Do you want me to light one for you?"

After thoroughly extinguishing the smoldering cigarette—it looked like something picked up in the aftermath of a fire—I pulled another one out of the pack. I hesitated for a moment, but decided to light it myself, then handed it to her.

"Here you are."

Our fingers touched slightly. The cigarette passed from my mouth to hers. For a while, she was completely absorbed in the enjoyment of her cigarette. I closed my eyes and listened. The room was so quiet I could hear the faint sound of the burning tobacco.

"You don't smoke?" Kyōko asked after some time passed.

"I smoke a pipe," I said, opening my eyes. "But in Japan, it's kind of tough because people look at you funny when they see a young person smoking a pipe."

She laughed. "Where'd you pick that up?"

"We have conscription in my country, so I was in the army for a while. I belonged to a tank corps to be exact. As part of our training, we often had to spend the entire night inside a tank. Now I'm talking about a really biting night in the middle of winter. So we'd pass a pipe around to feel a bit warmer. The smoke was incredible and we could hardly breathe, but somehow it worked. When you turn off the engine, a tank becomes as cold as the inside of a refrigerator."

She nodded without saying a word. My heart sank. I wondered how my story sounded to her, but I couldn't come up with the proper words to ask.

"As far as Japanese cigarettes are concerned," I continued, "My favorite are 'Shinsei.' They're like the French 'Gauloises.' They've got a real tobacco taste, and they're cheap. My philosophy on the subject is that cigarettes are deadly for your health to begin with. So if you're going to smoke, you might as well smoke something that's strong and has some flavor."

Kyōko felt for the ashtray, and flicked the ash off her cigarette. "A pipe, huh? That sounds fun. I'd like to try sometime," she said, as if speaking to herself.

During our reading breaks, we sometimes engaged in small talk or discussed literature as if we were young scholars of the Meiji Era. We discussed the content of books and exchanged naïve questions about literature. Though Kyōko couldn't actually read books, these conversations were very natural. Regardless of the genre or period, she was far more knowledgeable than I.

"Say, why would Ōta Toyotarō ever leave that cute dancer and want to return to Japan?" she said, looking extremely serious. "If it had been me, there's no way I would have chosen to go back to the boring life of a bureaucrat. I would've decided to live with my ballerina in Berlin. I'm sure he would have been happier watching her pursue her brilliant career as a star, while drinking German wine, and immersing himself in German literature."

"That does sound appealing. But I see him as a heartless guy with a hopeless mother complex who unfortunately couldn't break free from the bureaucratic system of the time. In his mind, moving up in his career was connected to pleasing his mother, and I don't think he had the stomach to go against that. Besides, he might not have been so keen about German wine."

Kyōko laughed. "I don't think you're really cut out to become a literary critic."

I laughed, too. "You're probably right."

We read many books as the early spring quietly passed by. Some we read from beginning to end, but mostly we just read sections of what I happened to have with me or of what I was studying at university.

There was a tall wooden bookcase in Kyōko's house. The bright colored Scandinavian-style clashed horribly with the Japanese-style living room, but it was stuffed with so many old books that my head spun.

"It's a bit musty, but don't you just love this coarse feel of the pages?" said Kyōko, pulling a book down from the shelf. "My mother bought this when she was young. Apparently, she used to be quite a bookworm." She handed me a book in a slightly faded green box.

It was Mori Tatsuo's *Kaze Tachinu* (The Wind Has Risen). I opened to the first page and found a short message written in the lower left corner: "To Yuriko, in fond memory of the days we shared in Karuizawa. From Ōsugi." Quite obviously, Kyōko's mother had been more than just an innocent literature lover. But I didn't say a word about this to Kyōko. Keeping her mother's little secret seemed but a small price to pay for the pleasure of sneaking through all these old books.

At the time, I was finally starting to get serious about my studies. I didn't have a clear vision of how that might connect to a future career or anything else, but I was really enthusiastic. During the day, I read in the university library or the small study room of the department of Japanese literature. I also attended all my lectures and seminars with regularity.

I studied not only on weekdays but also on weekends. I was what you might call a 24/7 student.

Shortly after I moved to Kyōto, the Kyōto International Exchanges Community House was built in the vicinity of my boarding house. The building was so luxurious that I couldn't help cynically thinking, "If you've got such a budget for international exchanges, why don't you use a little more of it to support foreign students?" But this didn't prevent me from spending all my weekends studying in the small library on the second floor.

In the evenings, I took a Hankyū or Keihan train to Ōsaka, where I had a tedious part-time job teaching English conversation. I worked for a small school that had its headquarters in Umeda and that dispatched teachers to various companies in Ōsaka and the surrounding area. Standing in front of the whiteboard of conference rooms, I taught English conversation to the male employees and so-called "office-ladies" or female office staff.

Some of the students were quite serious and well motivated, but others paid no attention and just wanted class to end as quickly as possible so that they could go out drinking with the teacher (it took me some time to get used to the fact that this word referred to me). I had to decide how to handle a class on the spur of the moment. To the average observer, it must have looked like a dream job: regardless of whether I taught well or poorly, my students were always happy and I received a salary. But to tell the truth, it was a hassle to commute to Ōsaka every night for an uninspiring job that provided absolutely nothing in return, apart from financial benefit.

The train ride took nearly an hour in each direction. Commuting back and forth, I experienced all kinds of situations. More often than not, they were unpleasant.

If I were reading a Japanese newspaper or novel while waiting for my train, about ninety-nine percent of the time, I'd have some kooky businessman sneak up from behind and spout out in an elated way, "Oh! You Japanese kanji okay?" Or some other gibberish.

I wanted to answer, "Mind your own business and leave me alone," but they were so darn insistent. After peeking over my shoulder for what seemed like an eternity, they'd reflect for a minute, and then come out with the ever-witty comment, "Japanese kanji *mu-zu-ka-shi-i*?"

Gosh… couldn't they come up with something other than the same old idioms over and over? In the first place, I wished they talked normally—in a non-discriminatory *normal* way.

I also ran into quite a number of strange characters while I was on the train. For instance, a businessman might sit down beside me and, after the train started moving, begin asking me all sorts of questions in English. I felt as if I were being interrogated by the police.

If I answered his questions in Japanese, he'd stand up while I was in the midst of my explanation and change his seat—as if to say, "I don't have time for foreigners who speak Japanese." Flabbergasted, I'd be left there with my mouth hanging open, looking like a complete idiot. I thought communication was a two-way street. Besides, we were in Japan, so shouldn't we have been speaking in Japanese? I could never tell whether such people truly wanted to speak with me or whether they just wanted to practice their English. Back then, I often got annoyed over this sort of thing.

Only my visits to Kurodani really liberated me from the faint gloom I felt at university and from the vain exhaustion of my part-time job. Before long, the place had become for me a treasured world of peace and serenity. I decided to keep this world jealously hidden from others. That's why I never spoke about Kyōko to the other foreign students or to any of my Japanese friends.

Just once, Nakayama-*san* from the foreign student lounge asked me, "So what happened with that blind girl?" I avoided the subject by vaguely answering, "Oh, her? I guess everything's going okay."

From the beginning of spring break, Kyōko and I started meeting on an almost daily basis. We didn't only read books, but also went on little dates. The first time we decided to go to town together, I was a bit confused. After our reading session, we agreed to go somewhere for dinner. I stepped out of the house first, and as I waited, I wondered how I was expected to escort her. Shortly after, she appeared in the doorway.

"Hey, don't you use one of those white canes when you go out?" I asked hesitantly as I gazed at the gravel pathway.

"Sure I do. I've got a fold-up cane in my bag. It's pretty cool. When I pull it out, it snaps out like a Karate weapon. That's why I call it my *nunchaku*." As she spoke, she tapped her shoulder bag lightly as if to let me know that one was inside.

"But if we're together, I don't need it, do I?" she said, lightly grasping my elbow with her fingertips. The message was clear; that's how I was to guide her.

"No, if we're together, I guess you don't," I answered.

We followed the winding road down to the Shirakawa-dōri street and boarded a bus in front of the Kinrin bus depot. The other passengers were staring at us. I felt extremely self-conscious as I guided Kyōko to a vacant seat. The combination of a foreign student with a young blind Japanese woman is probably too avant-garde for the people in this city, I thought as I sat down beside her. The scent of her perfume, a delicate mixture of vanilla and incense, wafted over to me.

We had tea in tearooms, watched movies in movie theaters, and did many other things. Needless to say, I was rather surprised the first time Kyōko suggested we go see a movie. But even though she couldn't see, she enjoyed the movies immensely. When it was a Japanese movie, I simply whispered short descriptions of the action and scenery to supplement the dialogue. But when it was a foreign movie, I also had to read all the subtitles, so things were much more difficult. On top of that, all my chattering would disturb those sitting nearby, so we had to sit far off to the side.

For no apparent reason, Kyōko would often lay her hand on my arm or nestle so close that our shoulders touched. For her, such gestures were extremely natural and had no special meaning. Yet every time she moved like that, I felt strangely confused.

I often used to explore the city on my own. My boarding house was near the Chion-in temple and Maruyama Park, and I loved gazing at Maruyama's cherry blossoms, lit up in the evening. The Shisen-dō hall was another one of my favorite spots. Once the cherry blossom season was over and tourists became scarce, I would spend hours looking at the garden, which reverberated with the rhythmical sound of a *shishi-odoshi* "deer-scarer" bamboo water pendulum. Sometimes I would head south to the Tōfuku-ji temples and enjoy the scenery of the Zen-style *tsuru-kame no niwa* Crane and Turtle Garden at the Sesshū-ji temple as I sipped *matcha* powdered green tea.

I would sit for ages on the wooden staircase at the Ryōan-ji temple admiring the stone garden. I could spend hours wandering around the Nanzen-ji temple, Kurama, the Nijō-jō castle, Arashiyama, Sagano, or the Heian-jingū shrine, without ever losing my sense of fascination. I tried to blend in with the city without analyzing anything. I cherished the appeasing timelessness of all the sceneries and works of architecture. Like a flat stone slowly sinking to the bottom of a slow-flowing stream, I gradually immersed myself in the purely Japanese ambiance of the place.

Without wondering even for a second why, I intensely desired something from Kyōto. I was trying to acquire, or perhaps to learn something from the city. For me, the old capital was a new frontier that offered the promise of discovery. And I longed to be accepted unconditionally. But aren't expectations often ruthless paths that lead to disappointment?

May was the season of school excursions.

Students from junior-highs and high-schools across the country descended on Kyōto like the dark swarms of locusts that periodically blanket entire areas of Africa. They would travel on foot or ride around on huge tourist buses that spewed foul-smelling exhaust fumes. The extravagant ones toured the city in luxury, using taxis. They all spent their days hunting for toy-like souvenirs and frantically taking souvenir photos of one another triumphantly flashing peace signs in front of temples or gardens they barely glanced at. When the sun went down, they could be seen squatting, absolutely exhausted, at the entrance of hotels or inns as they waited to be checked in.

Encountering one of these groups became a real nightmare. As soon as a student spotted me, he or she would immediately raise the alarm that a *gaijin*, or foreigner, had been spotted. The commotion would then spread through the entire horde like an infectious disease. "Hey, did you see that? There was a *gaijin*." "Where? Oh, you're right. I see him." "There he is, the *gaijin*!" "A *gaijin*, a *gaijin*... *gaijin*... *gaijin*... *gaijin.*"

I wanted to shout back at them, "Well sorry for being a *gaijin*!" But I was totally outnumbered, and before I knew it, they were all over me. Laugh about it, cry about it, there was no escape.

Then came the inevitable barrage of the one word gaijin were supposed to understand: "*Harō*! *Harō*! *Harō*! *Harō*!" Why couldn't Japanese schools teach their students how to pronounce "hello" properly? These mobs generally moved in groups of about a hundred (at least it felt that way to me), so quite a few salvos rained down on me during each onslaught. During the "season of the locusts," I was plagued by about a dozen attacks a day, so the total number of *harō*s must have been outrageously high—though I had no way of calculating the exact number.

Seen from the perspective of these young visitors, who were merely expressing their excitement, these encounters were probably no more than a few fleeting moments of their once-a-year school trip. But for me, exhausted by such repetitive yelling, the experience was absolutely unbearable.

It took but a few days before I had to struggle to suppress the anger and contempt I felt towards these students yelling, "*Gaijin*! *Harō*! *Harō*!" in the manner of programmed robots.

The rainy season fell upon us as if it had been lying in ambush. Rain poured down with a depressing consistency. The buildings in town, the asphalt of the streets, the old tiles on the roofs, and all other exposed objects became darkly stained by fat raindrops that fell endlessly. The city transformed itself into a tropical rain forest, where umbrellas replaced trees.

In no time, every conceivable object became soaked to the core. My old boarding house was a particularly disheartening disaster. The *tatami* mats became damp; the wallpaper became sticky as if dissolving into wet glue; and on the shelves, my books turned into rumpled and dejected figures.

The weather was truly detestable, but Steevie and Kyōko hated this steamy rainfall even more than I did. Steevie spent the entire day curled up in a corner of his box with an annoyed look on his face. His fur lost its luster, and he seemed to suffer a great deal from the heat and the humidity.

Kyōko, rather uncharacteristically, complained bitterly.

"Going to town during a downpour like this is just nightmarish," she explained. "It's so hard to know what's happening. You know, I rely on sound just as much as I do on touch. But when things get too loud, I get totally confused. There's the pouring rain, the cars swishing by on wet pavement, so many different sounds. And when they get jumbled up like this, it makes me lose my bearings. When I have something to carry, it's hard to hold my cane in one hand and an umbrella in the other. I almost wish I had an extra arm. My umbrella's always knocking into people and things, and their umbrellas are always banging me in the head as if seeking revenge. It's really awful." She grumbled in a frustrated tone.

I realized that being blind was far more problematic than what the average person could ever imagine. I nodded with sympathetic understanding. But of course Kyōko didn't notice.

At about that time, a friend who was a graduate school student began inviting me to sing karaoke late at night in a small bar in the Kiyamachi district.

According to rumor, the bar, which was located at the end of an alley that wound between closely packed buildings, had opened the very year the Beatles came to Japan. Its distinguishing feature was that the pictures on the walls, the videos projected on a large screen in the back, and even the LP jackets decorating the inside of the bathroom door were all memorabilia of the good old days of the Beatles.

Uehara-*san*, the owner, was a diehard Beatles fan. His original goal had been to have a quiet, relaxed place for fans to get together and chat about the group while listening to their favorite songs. His plan, however, completely fell apart. Years after setting the project in motion—actually just a little before we started going there—he committed an irreversible and fatal error: he purchased laser disc karaoke equipment and turned the place into a karaoke pub. His intention was to use the machine to project documentary footage of the Beatles on the large screen behind the counter. What happened, however, was that every time someone started singing, Paul McCartney immediately disappeared only to be replaced by one of those typically inane karaoke machine images. These ranged from splendid African nature shots to naked women writhing in ecstasy on heart-shaped beds. Whenever karaoke started, the owner would retreat deep behind his counter and sip whisky in silence.

The bar was extremely small, with no more than six or seven high stools around the narrow counter. Even by squeezing in more customers against the walls, packing in more than fifteen was a feat. As a result, the place was always as crowded as a rush-hour commuter train.

On Friday nights, there were many white-collar workers, mostly Beatles fans. Although I was from a different generation and country, they asked me many questions—at first in faltering English, then in Japanese. Their enthusiasm matched that of reporters pressing a repatriated soldier returning from battle for the latest news from the front.

Black clouds hung so low over the city that one could practically reach out and grab them. The end of the rainy season was close, but nonetheless, once a day a heavy downpour fell, just like a Southeast Asian squall.

When I arrived at the house in Kurodani, Kyōko was alone. I had barely settled down opposite her, when she abruptly announced in a mischievous tone, "How about reading something of mine today? You read nothing but Japanese literature these days, so I dug out this American novel for a change. Ta-da!"

The book she handed me was Anaïs Nin's *Henry and June*. As I took it in my hand, I was seized by mixed emotions. When I had first read the book—more or less on the sly—in high school, I had felt so excited I could hardly breathe and had to close my eyes more than once to calm myself. To me, the book was one of the most beautiful, sad, and erotic novels in contemporary fiction. The story of a complex relationship between three people ravenously pursuing sexual love and pleasure unfolds at a dizzying pace, and the tenderly passionate lesbian love scenes are more than enough to arouse a naïve high school student.

I swallowed so hard that the sound seemed to reverberate in the totally silent room.

"What's wrong? Don't you like Henry Miller?"

"I love Henry Miller," I said, opening *Henry and June* to an appropriate passage. "But I never imagined you'd have me read something like this."

It was my first time reading a foreign novel in Japanese translation. With a certain degree of apprehension, but also of curiosity, I began reading. As I did, two things occurred simultaneously: First, my voice became so hoarse it caught me by surprise. I felt peculiarly thirsty, and I had to clear my throat many times. Second, Kyōko quietly left her usual spot and edged very close to me. Facing my crossed legs, she stretched out on the *tatami* with her chin resting on her hand.

There were less than thirty centimeters between us. Conscious of my cracking voice and of Kyōko's presence just *too* near, I somehow managed to continue reading. Within five minutes, I reached the type of passage I had been dreading, a vivid description of the following scene:

In a dimly lit loft, Anaïs quietly slipped into June's bed. After straddling June's body, she unbuttoned her own pajama top, gently grasped June's hands, and pressed them against her breasts. As the force of Anaïs's hold gradually intensified, she began to waver with pleasure in silence. The two women's breathing grew shorter. Finally, Anaïs toppled forward, and rubbing her face like a kitten against June's opulent breasts, she began softly fondling her firm nipples with her thin lips. Henry was standing in the doorway, the faint moonlight penetrating the room from behind him. He projected a long shadow across the room, up to the edge of the bed. He had tears in his eyes.

That was the content of the passage. Before I realized it, I was reading silently to myself. An emotion quite different from the sexual excitement I had experienced long ago swept over me.

"Hey, what's the problem? That's not fair, stopping at a spot like that. I want to hear the juicy parts, too." Kyōko protested in the same mischievous tone as before.

I cleared my throat again. "Say, couldn't we perhaps read something else?" I proposed in a high-pitched voice. "This one's a bit… too much."

Kyōko disregarded my request. "Now don't tell me you're embarrassed. Are you blushing by any chance?" Kyōko laughed. "That's so cute. I never would have thought." She laid her hand lightly on my knee.

I couldn't find a word to reply.

"Listen," Kyōko said. "I really enjoy your reading to me, and I'm truly grateful. I mean it. But if you're going to do it, then no censorship! I want to enjoy these kinds of scenes as much as anyone else."

She did have a convincing argument. I swallowed hard again. There was a short silence. And as usual, the silence made me feel uncomfortable.

"Come on, please read a little more. And while we're at it, would you mind if I put my head on your lap?" Saying this, she subtly shifted her position and unaffectedly laid her head on my thigh.

Struggling to maintain my composure, I resumed reading. But my throat was completely dry. Carried by my voice, now merely a faint whisper, surrealistic and sensual phrases reached Kyōko's beautiful ear. She closed her eyes as if drifting into a world of pleasures that could not be seen but only spoken, and listened to the rest of the story.

Then the rain began to fall, as if faithfully fulfilling a promise made long ago. As we became engulfed by the gentle sound of rainfall, the scene in the loft from the novel and the actual living room we now occupied began to blend together—to the extent that I could barely distinguish them. I was terribly excited. The content of the book made me even more conscious of the weight and *closeness* of Kyōko's head on my lap. I felt something warm and sweet, but I couldn't determine whether the sensation came from within me or from Kyōko's body.

There was a particular sense of unity between the words on the paper, my voice reading them, and Kyōko silently listening. The print, my reciting, and the two of us no longer existed as distinct entities. I truly had the illusion that I was listening to somebody else's voice with Kyōko. Together, we peeked into the novel's deep sensuality, and together we were moved. Each sentence of the novel caused a subtle shift in the room's atmosphere, which began to take on a life of its own.

"This is so nice," Kyōko sighed, interrupting my reading. She smiled and opened her eyes again. For a moment, I had the feeling that she was indeed *looking* at me.

"Let's listen to the rain for a while," she whispered. "I've got a special talent for that. I can make out individual drops and tell where each one lands. Whether it's on the gravel path, or beating against the roof, or making a leaf sway… each has its own unique sound."

I focused all my senses on the rain. But I didn't have the ability to make out different sounds. However, concentrating on the rain like this seemed to quench the thirst in my throat.

I closed *Henry and June* and quietly laid it back on the *tatami*. The excitement I felt and the strange tension between Kyōko and me floated in the air. I could hardly repress the urge to put my hand on her shoulder. But our relationship was not of a nature that allowed such gestures.

Suddenly, without any warning, the rain stopped. It was almost eerie. After that, a mysterious silence fell over us. For a while, we sat absolutely still. The lingering effects of the novel and the rain prevented us from moving. The silence was totally different from the previous ones, and felt extremely comfortable. It was as if the calm after the storm had wrapped us in its embrace. I smiled to myself. Thinking about it, I realized that whenever I was with Kyōko, I always had this restless need to say something. It was as if I had unconsciously come to view silence as a sort of taboo, because of her blindness. I perhaps felt a need to fill the invisible with words.

But now, we were more comfortable without speaking. Within the silence, I sensed a definite form of communication—the content of which could not precisely be explained through words. We shared this wordless conversation for what seemed like ages.

After the rainy season, the area along the Takasegawa river became suffocatingly hot and muggy. Even so, every weekend the area between the Sanjō-dōri and Shijō-dōri avenues teemed with sweat-drenched college students carrying on with amazing energy. On the other side of the Kamogawa river were exclusive clubs and expensive teahouses—surrounded by gay bars and strip joints. It was the world of Gion, where the foul smell of fraudulent money was everywhere. Our karaoke group had nothing to do with that world. Our favorite place was still the small Beatles bar, where we could sing cheaply and drink whisky until morning. I practiced many songs and drank massive quantities of alcohol there. Foreign students from China, Korea, Brazil, and other countries also sometimes joined us. I tried singing all kinds of songs, including the Southern All Stars, Alice, Nagabuchi Tsuyoshi, Sada Masashi, and Inoue Yōsui. The next step was then to work on brushing up my repertoire.

We usually left the bar after watching the 5 a.m. NHK News. Of course, it was getting light outside by that time. After spending an entire night in semi-darkness, even the faint early morning light seemed unbelievably bright. In the northern part of Kiyamachi was a small *rāmen* noodle shop. It was so popular, that even in the early morning, people would queue patiently outside. Not quite sobered up yet, we squatted in front of the shop and ate *kimchi rāmen* in the pale morning sunlight. I had a hard time squatting, so I usually ate standing up. Nevertheless, the spicy hot *kimchi rāmen* we ate in the fresh morning breeze, after a long night singing and drinking, tasted out of this world.

After that, we headed to the banks of the Kamogawa river, sat down on the hard flagstone overlooking the shallow current, and continued our rambling conversations. The area near the Sanjō-Ōhashi bridge was surprisingly crowded, mostly with other students who had spent the night in a similar way to us, but also with lovers who had whispered sweet things to each other until dawn—without finding a way to satisfy their sexual appetite. These couples sat side-by-side facing the river, spaced out at intervals that seemed to have been measured with a ruler. As for me, I felt extremely calm and somewhat detached from everything. I just enjoyed the sensation of *kimchi rāmen* and whisky mixing in my body.

After meeting Kyōko and beginning my new *job* as a "face-to-face" reader several times a week, I had spent a relatively productive spring as a foreign student. But when summer arrived in earnest and I could no longer endure the heat of the Kyōto basin, I decided to leave town and hitchhike to Hokkaidō. As with my past travels, it was a penniless journey that could have been the basis for an article in a *Lonely Planet* travel guide. I didn't have the financial leeway to stay in a hotel or a *ryokan* Japanese-style inn, and I didn't want to bother with the troublesome rules of a Japanese youth hostel, so I stuffed an old tent and a sleeping bag in my knapsack, and moved around like a fugitive.

Japan was literally a hitchhiker's paradise. I stood on the side of the road holding a cardboard sign that read "Heading to Hokkaidō," a concise message indicating my direction, and it usually wouldn't take more than five minutes for a car to stop. Everyone was extremely friendly—except for a few rare cases.

Was it because they didn't understand the concept of hitchhiking? On two occasions (to be precise, once in a small nameless country town in Shizuoka, and once in Kōriyama, a city in Fukushima Prefecture), I was picked up, but only to be immediately dropped off again at the nearest station and urged to board a train. Another time (between Morioka and Aomori), a strange man driving an old-fashioned Nissan Cherry asked—in the same tone one would use when inquiring about the odds at a horse race—"If you strangled someone with all your strength, how long do you think it'd take for him to die?" There was also a rich elderly woman driving a red Alfa Romeo. She took me on the ferry to Hakodate, treated me to a nice dinner at a restaurant overlooking the lights of the city, and then tried desperately to drag me to a hotel with her.

But such incidents are only part of the hitchhiking game, and the rest of my trip went smoothly. I traveled the most in large-sized trucks that stopped for me regularly. I'd had the same experience in many other countries. For a trucker who's bored driving, picking up a foreign hitchhiker is a welcome change. It provides the entertainment of hearing about foreign countries *first-hand*, as well as an opportunity to receive free foreign cigarettes. Seen from my point of view, as trucks usually travel long distances in one go, I was able to make good mileage. In other words, it was a decent deal for both sides.

Sitting next to the driver and watching Hokkaidō's breath-taking landscapes from the vantage point of my high seat was exhilarating. I spent nearly a month traveling around Kushiro Marsh, Shiretoko Peninsula, Lake Kussharo, Wakkanai City, and Daisetsuzan National Park. I certainly did pitch my tent in quite a variety of places. Along the way, shaving became a nuisance, so I decided to let my beard grow.

CHAPTER TWO

When I returned a month later, Kyōto seemed to have lost much of its charm. The early September air was outrageously hot and muggy. But that could barely have been the only cause for the change I felt. It was as if the city was revealing a totally unknown face to me.

Since I couldn't figure out whether the city had actually changed, or if my emotions were altering my perception, I decided I might as well go pick up Steevie. While I was in Hokkaidō, a friend in the English literature department had taken care of him.

This friend lived directly behind the university. His apartment was on the second floor of a *sentō* and had that distinct bathhouse smell. Though he lived about an hour's walk from my boarding house, I decided to take a stroll and go on foot. As I followed the Shirakawa river towards the Heian-jingū shrine, I noticed swarms of bugs above the surface. In the distance, a heron stood seemingly transfixed with its thin legs in the shallow water. Perhaps the oppressive heat of the city was generating bizarre mirages. The huge gateway to the Heian-jingū shrine bore the full brunt of the afternoon sun, and its towering mass glowed bright red, as if pleading to some divinity for an escape from the unbearable heat.

Walking in the muggy afternoon air did nevertheless yield some reward: as I trudged along, I gradually gained an insight into the source of my negative feelings towards my surroundings.

It was an urban scenery problem.

All year long, hordes of tourists from Japan and throughout the world visited Kyōto. There were those silly Japanese students who couldn't resist yelling, "Hey, *gaijin*! *Harō*! *Harō*!" There were fat Americans wearing shorts and gaudy t-shirts. There were middle-aged Japanese men with fancy cameras mounted on tripods trying to take the *perfect* Kyōto photograph. Then there were young couples who spent the daytime sightseeing and the night in the *love-hotels* of the Keage district. All sorts of people came to Kyōto with all sorts of expectations. These students on school trips, world travelers, and mildly indecent lovers each in their own way admired the temples, shrines, buildings, and scenes that still retained some vestiges of their former glory.

But seen from an urban landscape perspective, the place was totally chaotic. The dense jungle of telephone poles resembled the American countryside from the old days of the Wild West. No matter where you looked, the arrangement of buildings was woefully disharmonious. You might find a long-established antique store sandwiched between a pachinko parlor and a karaoke joint. Or wooden houses, concrete structures, and apartment buildings of all sorts and sizes standing unconcernedly in a row. The city sometimes even seemed grotesque. Comparing such scenery to the majestic and awesome landscapes of Hokkaidō only made the impression stronger.

It's not that I hated clutter or confusion. Given the choice, I preferred a certain degree of chaos. But chaos should generate energy. And on this early afternoon of September, Kyōto seemed simply far too lethargic, its twelve-hundred-year history just too stagnant for my taste.

Steevie greeted me with a look of *total* indifference to the problem. The heat having taken its toll, he had lost weight. He had a peevish expression, which also revealed his annoyance at having been abandoned to a total stranger—who didn't even own a fan or an air conditioner. My friend, in contrast, couldn't hide his relief. "I love animals," he said, "but taking care of a rabbit in this small room is really a hassle. I nearly got kicked out by my landlord."

"Sorry about that," I said, my smile probably unconvincing. I handed him the souvenir t-shirt I had bought in Hokkaidō. "I owe you one." I then took the box with my flustered rabbit, boarded the taxi my friend had called for me, and returned home.

I decided to spend the rest of my summer break lounging around in my room. I slid the window open, gave Steevie some food and water, and for the first time in a long time, pulled a book from the shelf. It was the *Collected Works of Tayama Katai*. Opening to a page at random, I began reading *Ippeisotsu no Jūsatsu* (A Soldier Shot to Death), a novel written in 1917.

Sitting in front of the window with the afternoon sun beating on my back, I read the story of the young soldier's lonely and pathetic death. As I read, a strange phenomenon occurred—a subtle change in my feelings, unrelated to the book's content. As I immersed myself in Tayama's story, I felt Kyōko's presence settling over me—like a butterfly gently alighting on a flower.

I finished the novel within three hours or so. The afternoon sun had sunk low, but it was still pretty hot. I stood up and closed the window, returned the *Collected Works of Tayama Katai* to the bookcase, and went outside. For some mysterious reason, I had a strong desire to take a walk to Kyōko's neighborhood.

As I strolled though the evening streets, a cool breeze began to blow. I was glad that I had decided to go for a walk. After about fifteen minutes,

I approached the winding hill that led to the gate with the thatched roof. A woman wearing a kimono appeared. It was Kyōko's mother. I wasn't that surprised to see her. After all, she was one of the two women I'd been hoping to run into. Or to be more precise, the moment I spotted her, I was made aware of the motives that had led me there.

"Good evening. It's been a while."

"Oh, my! Good evening. Yes it has been a long time! And you've returned with a beard! You look so different, I hardly recognized you. When did you get back?"

After a moment of confusion, she quickly recovered and greeted me in the same warm voice as before.

"The beard I acquired in Hokkaidō. I returned the day before yesterday, and since I was taking a walk, I decided to stop by and say hello." Feeling nervous for some reason, my explanation had the formal tone of a university presentation.

"Well, then, please do stop by for a visit. I'm sure Kyōko would be thrilled. I'm going to do some shopping, so please go ahead without me."

She began walking towards the Shirakawa-dōri street again, and I began climbing the small hill in the opposite direction. But she suddenly called my name, so I turned around.

"If you haven't eaten, why don't you stay and have dinner with us? We'd love to hear about your trip to Hokkaidō."

Thirty minutes later, we were stepping through the small gate with the thatched roof, both of us carrying groceries in our hands.

Kyōko was sitting on the veranda wearing a dark blue tank top and a short skirt, as befitted the summer. It was the first time I saw her legs. They were slender and inviting. "Morning Moonlight," a love song by the Southern All Stars, was playing in the living room. The title didn't match the time of day, but the melody suited the scene so perfectly you'd think it had been composed expressly for this precise moment. The soothing air rustled through the room. Kyōko, sitting as if giving herself to the breeze, looked supremely refreshed. Apparently having caught the sound of our footsteps on the gravel, she turned towards us.

"Mother, who is it?"

I approached awkwardly, still holding the groceries. Kyōko turned slightly in my direction.

"Kyōko, it's been a while. How've you been?"

She must have recognized my voice, but she didn't say a word. Instead, she slowly and deliberately brushed back the strands of hair that had blown in her face, and then remained perfectly still. A song unknown to me began to play.

"It was an extremely hot and humid summer," she said, sounding like an elementary school teacher scolding a pupil. "It's most inappropriate that you should return only after it finally gets cool. You'll never truly understand Japanese culture if you don't experience Kyōto's summer." She then put out her hand and smiled. "But I forgive you. Welcome back."

It was the first time she tried to shake hands with me. I took her hand, while being careful not to drop the groceries.

"It's still hot enough to get a fairly good idea of Japanese culture," I said, laughing.

The three of us had dinner in the small living room. It was dark outside, and we couldn't see the garden. Cans of beer and various dishes of food were set out on the "naked" *kotatsu*, now devoid of its quilting. The scent of a burning mosquito coil drifted from the corner. Kyōko, wearing a reddish brown cardigan over her tank top, was obviously enjoying herself.

I was surprised by how deftly she handled her chopsticks. She'd touch the edge of the dish with the ends, locate the position of the food, and then effortlessly carry each morsel to her mouth. Such dexterity was probably to be expected, but I was impressed.

"Kyōko, is there anything you can't eat with chopsticks?"

"I can handle most things, but the most difficult is—." She put down her chopsticks and gave the question some thought. "I guess fish with lots of bones give me the most trouble. And also crab. People take an incredibly long time eating crab, don't they? Well, it takes me about three times longer than average. I'm a burden to everyone whenever I eat out."

As we ate, I spoke about my trip to Hokkaidō. Kyōko, however, didn't seem very interested. What fascinated her was to hear about my beard, and all her questions focused on that. So I told her all about how I had grown it—even though there wasn't much to explain.

When her mother cleared the table and left the room, Kyōko rested her elbows on the *kotatsu* tabletop and leaned forward.

"You know, I've never actually touched a man's beard before," she said in a mischievous tone of voice. "Would you mind if I touched yours?"

"By all means, go ahead. This week we're offering a special free trial on beard touching. Hurry! Hurry and touch as much as you like," I said, mimicking those bargain sale announcements that bombard you at supermarkets.

"That peculiar sense of humor of yours hasn't changed," she said with a smile. Then she slightly tilted her head to the side, reached out her hand, and hesitantly searched for my face. "Sorry, everyone says I'm too curious for words."

"A little over this way."

I took her hand and gently pressed it against my beard. She caressed it with the back of her hand. Slightly frowning and with her head turned downward, she concentrated on the sensation. Looking at such an intent expression, I couldn't help laughing.

"Stay still," she said, cradling my chin in her hand to prevent me from moving.

The way she stroked my beard subtly changed: the movement of her slender fingers grew gentler, and her face, with her eyes half-closed, edged close to mine. I was flustered, which always happens when a woman's face comes close to mine. Her full, shapely lips were much too close. She didn't say a word, and I didn't say anything either. The next thing I knew, her hand had stopped moving.

For an instant, time came to a halt.

Caught in the moment, I softly kissed her lips—barely conscious of what I was doing. Her hand didn't leave my face. Our lips had only lightly touched, and only for a split second. I couldn't believe it. Yet a definite aftertaste remained on my lips, and there was no doubt that we had indeed shared a short kiss.

She backed away about two centimeters.

"Is that also part of the special free trial?" she asked with a smile. Her breath was warm and smelled of frothy beer.

I wanted to say something witty, but I couldn't come up with anything. Just then, I heard the footsteps of Kyōko's mother returning from the kitchen.

"Well, it's rather quiet in here," she said. "I brought some watermelon for dessert." Her crisp voice made the kiss seem all the more unreal.

As we ate the fresh fruit, Kyōko acted as if nothing had happened. Struggling to somehow pull myself together, I focused on eating my watermelon in silence. When we finished, Kyōko's mother gathered the rinds together on a plate, stood up, and headed back to the kitchen.

When we were alone again, Kyōko felt for the tape player and pressed the play button. A Southern All Stars song that I didn't know began to play. Singing to the music, she pulled a rubber band from her sweater pocket and tied her hair back in a ponytail. She had an enchanting voice.

I wanted to kiss her again. What was the meaning of that first one? I was completely baffled. Kissing her again might have provided valuable information, but the atmosphere didn't seem conducive to resuming where we had left off.

"You've got a really good voice, Kyōko," I said instead, giving up on the idea of a kiss. "Do you enjoy singing like this?"

She nodded. "When I lived in Tōkyō, I used to go to karaoke with my friends from the transcription group. I can't see the monitor, so I have to memorize the lyrics. But I do think I have some talent." She sounded quite proud of herself.

"Well I'd say you do," I said, thinking of the Beatles bar my friends and I frequented. "Hey, there's this small karaoke place in Kiyamachi where I go from time to time. Would you like to join me next time?"

"Sure, I'd love to," she said.

Later in the evening, I left Kyōko's house and wandered home the way I had come. By the time I got back, the *sentō* had already closed, but I didn't care in the least.

The month of September was peculiarly hot. Over the next couple of days, the other students living in the boarding house returned one by one. The place became noisy again—and in no time turned into a pigsty. A student from the ground floor told me he had gone to China during the summer holidays. That fall, he spent nearly every day working loudly and with determination on his Chinese pronunciation—with the front window of his room half open.

The guy living directly beneath me had found himself a girlfriend over the summer. I never actually met her, though she came to his room nearly every day. In the evening, I could sometimes hear their conversation through the thin floor. As time passed, however, the chit-chat grew scarcer, to be replaced by rather explicit moaning sounds. There are many people in the world, and many ways of spending summer holidays.

Within the grounds of the boarding house was an old traditional *kura* storage house. When the group of students who lived there returned, the small room on the second floor resumed its function as a hangout for a bunch of grungy-looking guys. Apparently, their only pleasure in life was to play mahjong until the crack of dawn. It's all well and fine that different people should get their kicks from different activities. But I personally felt more sympathy for the fellow deepening an intimate relation with a mysterious girlfriend than for these guys crammed into a tiny room playing mahjong and puffing away on cigarettes day and night.

One day, I woke up extra early, washed my face, and went straight out.

I entered the Mister Donut shop on the corner of Sanjō-dōri and Higashiōji-dōri avenues and promptly ordered coffee, orange juice, one Twist, two Honey Dips, and one Sugar Raised donut. Though I had ordered in Japanese, the girl at the counter mumbled in stilted English, "You take out, or eat here?" A bit annoyed, I fired back, "*Tennai de tabemasu,*" I'll be eating here.

As I chomped on my donuts, I flipped through my memo book. Soon after the break, I had to make some important presentations. Scrawled on the page were the following notes:

—Survey of Modern Chinese Literature
Discuss pro-Americanism in the short stories of Lao She
—Special Topics 4
List and analyze the differences in the original manuscript, standard edition, and revised edition of Shimazaki Tōson's *Yoakemae* (Before the Dawn)
—Seminar on Modern Literature
Trace the inevitability of Takeo and Namiko's tragedy in Tokutomi Roka's *Hototogisu* (The Cuckoo)

This abrupt confrontation with reality was disconcerting. I closed my notebook in a slight state of panic. The coffee in the bottom of the cup was as alluring as a puddle on a summer glacier. I shoved the notebook back in my pocket and left.

The morning air was still abnormally hot, and reminded me of Kyōko's comment about Kyōto having become cooler. I yearned to see her. But as I wasn't able to come up with a convincing excuse for doing so, I got on my scooter and headed to the university instead.

Without students, the campus seemed as deserted as a baseball stadium during the off-season. No one was in *Dejima* either, so I headed to the seminar room, located on the top floor of another building. The room had one large square table, surrounded by numerous bookcases. I opened the large window facing north and let the cool air fill the room.

First, I went to the modern literature stacks towards the back and found a copy of Tokutomi Roka's *The Cuckoo*. The thin Iwanami paperback felt enticing in my hands. I figured I could breeze through it in three days.

After reading the first few lines, however, my confidence was shattered. The style was unbelievably difficult. I sighed heavily.

I looked out the window. The spacious sky was dizzyingly blue and tauntingly transparent. I pondered the infinite pitch-dark reaches of the universe that stretched out behind it. I opened my memo book again and checked to see how long I had until the presentations. Nearly three more weeks. No need to panic. Relieved, I looked outside again.

Why does the sky look blue even though outer space is pitch-black? I certainly must have received a rudimentary explanation back in elementary school. But in those days, just like now, I spent all my time looking out the window, so I probably missed it. There are ironic moments in life where our actions work at cross purposes to our desires.

I ended up spending the entire day in idleness.

I so desperately wanted to see Kyōko that my desire robbed me of any ability to concentrate. I gave her a call when I got back to the boarding house later that evening, but quite unexpectedly, it was Kyōko's mother who answered.

"Kyōko went to town. She said she wouldn't be back before nine."

Her voice had its usual youthful ring. But I was disappointed that Kyōko wasn't home.

"So, should I have her call you when she returns?" she asked, sounding suspicious of my conspicuous silence.

"Uh, yes, please," I answered nervously.

When I hung up, I realized I was famished. I hadn't eaten a thing all day, other than the donuts I'd had for breakfast. Worried that Kyōko might call, I decided to change the answering machine message before leaving. On the assumption she'd call, I put on Janet Kay's "Lovin' You" for background music and recorded a brief message: "Tonight, I'm having *miso champon* and *gyōza* for supper. I should be back in an hour, so please be sure to try again."

I often ate at a small Chinese restaurant called Sanpō Hanten, which was near the boarding house. In addition to Szechuan-style shrimp in chili sauce, spicy ground meat and tofu, sweet and sour pork, and the other ordinary dishes Chinese joints offer anywhere in Japan, Sanpō Hanten also served the somewhat unusual *miso champon*. This was a *miso*-flavored *rāmen* soup with thick noodles heaped with vegetables, shrimp, and squid.

An extra large *miso champon*, *gyōza* dumplings, and a beer—certainly not very healthy, but that was my favorite order. Wolfing down the steaming hot *champon* at a speed that risked blistering my mouth and then washing it down with big swigs of beer always brought me a tremendous sense of satisfaction.

At the back of the shop was an enormous air conditioner unit coated with oil and dust. It was so old you felt tempted to attach a label saying, "Special exhibit: early post-war electrical appliance." Above the unit was a small red television set, which was halfway through a variety show when I started eating. I watched the show as I slurped up my *miso champon*.

As with many other foreign students, I found television a valuable instrument for studying Japanese. I had often watched the late-night news as part of my entrance exam preparations. It took nearly two years before I could follow the gist of the rapidly speaking newscasters.

On the Sanpō Hanten TV, which had horrible reception, a famous personality was twisting his head back and forth nervously and making his neck pop. His gesture reminded me of the courtship rituals of the cockatoos I had once seen deep in the jungles of Sri Lanka. The guy tossed out another lame joke, and the TV audience and everyone in the shop broke out laughing.

When I returned to the boarding house, the lamp on my answering machine was flashing joyously. My heart slightly pounding, I pressed the play button.

"Hello, it's Kyōko. I've never heard of *miso champon*. Are you putting me on? Next time, you'll have to take me with you. I'll be up late, so give me a call when you get in."

As soon as the message finished playing, I dialed her number. She answered right away. Without the slightest hesitation, I said, "I wasn't kidding about *miso champon*. In fact, I just polished off a bowl for supper."

"Is that right? So it does exist," she answered, sounding impressed.

"Sure it does. Hey, what kept you out so late?"

"Drinking in Teramachi with friends." Her intonation was strained, and she seemed to have problems articulating.

"Drinking? Oh, you drink?" I asked in surprise.

"Anything wrong with that?" she replied with a pretence of sulkiness in her voice.

"No, nothing. Nothing at all."

There was a short pause.

"Anyhow, I'm still a bit tipsy, so please don't talk about anything complicated."

I tried to picture her in an inebriated state, but I couldn't.

"Don't worry. I'm a bit out of it, too, from the *miso champon* and beer. I couldn't talk about anything complicated if I wanted to."

A silence of about five seconds followed.

"To tell the truth… I was hoping… to take you to that karaoke bar. The one I told you about. Would you like to go?"

"Sure, I'd love to," she answered sounding quite thrilled.

"So when would be a good time?"

"I had too much to drink today, so I'll need a break tomorrow. How about Friday?"

"Okay. I haven't started my part-time job yet, so I've got lots of free time. Whenever suits you."

"Let's settle for Friday, then. Listen, I don't know the place, so could you come by here, so we can go together?"

"Sure thing. I'll stop by on Friday at six. Try to sober up and get yourself together by then."

"No problem. I've got almost forty hours to get ready."

I smiled.

"Well, that's a relief. I'm looking forward to seeing you when you're feeling better. So I guess I'd better say good night." I really wanted to talk longer, but I couldn't think of what to say, so I figured I'd better hang up.

Kyōko didn't respond.

"Hey, hello? Anything wrong?"

"No nothing. Nothing at all… Good night."

She really did sound tipsy. I smiled and slipped the receiver back in its cradle.

On Friday, it rained lightly on and off all day. Unfortunately one could say, yet as a result, when at six o'clock I was standing in front of Kyōko's house with a large umbrella, it had cooled off a bit. Kyōko appeared with her hair tied back in a ponytail with a purple hair band, just as on the day I had first laid eyes on her. The hairstyle, which nicely displayed her long neck and delicately shaped ears, suited her well. A pair of gold earrings dangled from her ears, and she was in jeans. Over a white t-shirt with a large cartoon-like frog, she wore a thin mauve cardigan and an expensive-looking gold chain necklace.

"I don't look strange, do I?" she asked anxiously.

"Not at all. You look very elegant."

"It's really hard choosing clothes without knowing their color you know."

"I can imagine, but your outfit is very becoming." The combination of gold and purple was also pleasing to the eye, so I complemented her again.

I noticed that the lights were out, which made the house look deserted.

"Isn't your mother home?"

"No," Kyōko said, locking the front door. "She's visiting relatives in Tōkyō for the next few days. So no curfew, which suits me fine." This remark, although stated in a nonchalant way, made me wonder if Kyōko ever yearned for more freedom. The rain, which had stopped for a while, started falling again. I tugged Kyōko lightly by the arm and pulled her under the umbrella.

We got off the bus at the Sanjō Kawaramachi intersection and headed south along the Takasegawa river. As usual, Kyōko held my arm lightly above the elbow and walked diagonally behind me. Everyone we passed turned around and gawked.

Finally, we entered an alley that led to the Kawaramachi-dōri street, where there was an *okonomiyaki* Japanese-style pancake restaurant called "Come Again." The place was packed, and there was so much smoke from the grilling hot plates and cigarettes you could hardly see the interior. I held up two fingers to the waitress and said, "*Futari desu,*" two of us. We were guided to seats at the counter in the back.

I ordered two large mugs of draft beer. The menu was handed over with the beers.

"Well, we've got our drinks, so I'd like to propose a toast," I said, pushing one of the mugs in front of Kyōko. She felt for the handle and lifted the beer with effort.

"What should we drink to?"

"World peace is a little banal, but it'll do for now."

I clinked my mug lightly against hers.

"To world peace!"

We took long quaffs and wiped the foam from our mouths with the back of our hands almost simultaneously. After that, we ordered one green onion *negiyaki* and one *okonomiyaki* with shrimp. The man behind the counter applied oil to the hot plate in front of us and began mixing the ingredients with two small spatulas.

“I’ve always wanted to work in an *okonomiyaki* restaurant,” I said, leaning against Kyōko. “It must be great cooking in front of people like this.”

She gently pushed back against me, and I felt the roundness of her shoulder beneath her cardigan.

“You can cook?” she asked.

I took another sip of beer.

“Don’ sell me shor’ when’t comes to cookin’.”

“And why shouldn’t I *sell ya shor’*?” asked Kyōko, mimicking my bungling Kansai dialect.

“I don’t mean to brag, but when I was in high school, I used to work in an *auberge* in southern France during the summer holidays.”

“Like, what’s an *auberge*?” asked Kyōko, suddenly switching to the dialect of a Yokohama high school girl.

“It’s a kind of laid-back gourmet restaurant. I worked there for two months a year and learned quite a bit about cooking. It’s really great to know how to cook, and certainly very practical. Good food has universal appeal, doesn’t it? So if you can cook, you’re bound to find a job anywhere. When I traveled around the world on a ship, I worked in the kitchen.”

“You traveled around the world on a ship?” asked Kyōko in surprise.

“That’s right. I grew up in the mountains, so I always wanted to see the ocean. A captain I met in that restaurant in France offered me a job, so I worked as part of his crew for a year. That was the first time I visited Japan.”

“Wow! Is that how it happened?” Kyōko seemed quite impressed.

The man behind the grill slid the *negiyaki* and the *okonomiyaki* in front of us with his spatulas.

“Let’s eat,” I said, cutting up my *okonomiyaki* with my spatula. Kyōko snapped her wooden *waribashi* disposable chopsticks apart and began eating as skillfully as at dinner the other night. The way she handled chopsticks struck me as nothing short of amazing, no matter how often I saw it.

“How about making us something nice for dinner some time?”

“Gee, I don’t know. Come to think of it, I haven’t done much cooking since I settled down here. I don’t have much money, and it’s tough to find the right ingredients. Besides, you wouldn’t want me to cook in the kitchen where I live. You’d be sure to get food poisoning.”

“Is that right?” Kyōko looked disappointed, but a moment later, she had a big smile on her face. “You know what? Why don’t you come to our house and cook?" she said, making a constructive proposal. "Our kitchen is impeccably clean."

We were eating and drinking at a good pace, and both our *okonomiyaki* and beer were soon gone. Cool droplets dribbled down the side of our mugs.

It had stopped raining by the time we left. Across the street, a huge neon sign that read "Pink's Peep Show" was flashing. In front of the club, a middle-aged man wearing a tuxedo was soliciting customers. He gave us a suspicious glance and abruptly turned his head in the opposite direction. Apparently people in this town viewed us as strange. When I was alone, such blatant displays of hostility made me uncomfortable, but when I was with Kyōko, somehow they didn't bother me.

We arrived at the Beatles bar. When we pushed the wooden door open, the owner was mixing a cocktail behind the counter. He didn't notice us, but the four customers already seated at the counter immediately turned their gazes in our direction. For a split second, I felt a strong impulse to run away. Thankfully, the owner noticed the strange silence and lifted his head.

"Sorry, I didn't see you," he said, beckoning us to enter. "Come on in!"

We sat down at two empty seats against the wall. When he noticed me take the proffered *oshibori* freshly damped napkin-towel and press it into Kyōko's hand, he realized she was blind. An awkward silence hung in the air as we wiped our hands, but I promptly and cheerfully said, "This is my friend, Kyōko." The owner immediately regained his usual friendly expression and bowed.

"Pleased to meet you. I'm Uehara. Thanks for coming."

I ordered two Jack Daniels on the rocks, and we had another toast.

After we drank and chatted for a while, I picked up the mike and whispered to Kyōko, "I'm going with a somber lineup tonight."

When I started singing *Tombo* (The Dragonfly) the bar suddenly became quiet, and everyone stared. Out of the corner of my eye, I noticed some guy pumping the owner for information, but I went on singing. Kyōko sipped her whisky, and listened with her head tilted to the side. As I sang, I stared at her beautifully shaped ear. I strongly desired to send her a message. But I couldn't figure out how or what exactly it was, so I just stared at her ear and kept singing.

When the song was over, the bar erupted in applause that bordered on overkill. The man sitting nearby leaned from his stool and slapped me on the back. "You're absolutely incredible! Truly amazing! Out of this world!"

"It's thanks to Uehara-*san*," I explained. "He lets me practice here whenever I want." But the man wasn't listening. He had already turned away to harangue someone else with his monologue.

"Truly incredible! Never in my life have I heard a foreigner sing like that! Unbelievable! Japan has really changed!"

This comment triggered a barely audible debate concerning the internationalization of Japan. The debate didn't last long, however, and when the next song started, the man who had praised me scurried off to grab the mike and soon lost himself in an *enka* song I didn't know. Actually, as I hated the melodramatic sentimentality of these songs so popular with middle-aged men, the number of *enka* I knew was close to nil.

I finished my drink and ordered another. Kyōko seemed to be dozing off with her chin resting on her hand.

"Kyōko, are you okay?" I asked, putting my hand on her arm. "You're not drunk, are you?"

"I thought you had forgotten all about me," she said, as if sulking. While I was struggling to come up with an answer, she continued, "But you sang really well. I'm impressed." Then she nudged her head, still resting in her hand, against my shoulder.

"Thanks."

For a moment, her head weighed against my shoulder. It was a pleasant heaviness. To be more accurate, it was the perfect weight you'd expect for Kyōko's head. A light perfume scent, mingled with the smell of *okonomiyaki*, wafted towards me.

Before long, the man finished his song, but hardly anyone applauded.

"Here you are, Kyōko," said the owner, handing her the mike. "Sorry to have kept you waiting." Another song began to play.

When she began singing, the owner stopped drying beer glasses and stood rooted to the spot, his mouth hanging half open. The customers also grew still and stared in blank amazement. Her eyes half closed, Kyōko sang without hesitation or conceit, a surrealistic picture of beauty and mystery.

Her softly protruding breasts undulated below the gold chain necklace as the frog on her chest moved with each breath. I gasped and gazed spellbound. When she finished, not a soul stirred, and an indescribable hush fell over the bar. If someone had entered at that very precise moment, he'd probably never have imagined it was a karaoke bar.

Kyōko felt for the counter and put down the mike. A screeching metallic sound came from the speakers. As if that were the signal, the bar burst into thunderous applause. Kyōko's carefree expression changed into an endearing look of confusion.

When the applause died down, a fat middle-aged man ordered another whisky and water in a loud voice. "Uehara, give me another!" he said. "The singing's so good tonight I can hardly get drunk!"

A couple of young "office ladies" also pushed forward their glasses, and chimed in unison, "We wanna 'nother, too!" After that, however, the barflies paid no heed to us and returned to their own isolated conversations.

Soft Beatles music played for a while. I laid my hand lightly on Kyōko's forearm.

"I'm the one who's impressed, Kyōko," I said, hardly able to contain my excitement.

She placed her other hand over mine and smiled.

"It's incredible that you could remember the lyrics for such a difficult song."

"It's really quite simple," she said, making it sound really quite easy. "Once I hear a song, it usually just sticks in my head."

"That's all there is to it?"

She raised her glass to take another drink, but it was empty. Small chunks of melting ice came tumbling against her lips. With the Beatles' "Anna (Go to Him)" playing in the background, the sound of ice clinking against the glass sounded nice.

"Hey, it's empty," said Kyōko, with the ice cubes still resting on her lips.

"May I pour you another?" asked Uehara-*san*, kindly coming to the rescue.

"Yeah, I wanna 'nother," she said, mimicking the tone of the office ladies before.

"Anna (Go to Him)" was still playing when it suddenly happened. We were talking about the Beatles, I think, but that's not really important. In the excitement of the conversation, our hands gently brushed together. Uncertain, I was about to pull my hand away, but Kyōko entwined her fingers in mine. She left them like that as our conversation continued, occasionally softly caressing my hand with the tips of her fingers.

The music, people's conversations, glasses clicking together—every sight and sound became blurry and faded into mist. I don't know how long the sensation continued, but when I returned to my senses, the customers at the next table were paying their bill. On his way out, the fat middle-aged man who had sung *enka* glanced over at me and then sarcastically muttered, "You really gotta wonder where our country's heading."

The comment jolted me back to reality. "It's not heading anywhere, you fart," I blurted out. Kyōko burst out laughing, and whisky spilled from her glass. She edged close to me again, and said, "Don't pay him any attention. He's a relic from another generation."

We were both quite drunk by the time we left. The evening air was invigorating, and since there was no sign of rain, we decided to walk a bit. Kyōko slid her arm under mine, and we walked side by side. We hardly spoke a word. We cut through the Pontochō-dōri street, crossed the Shijō-hashi bridge, and passed the Minamiza kabuki theater. After making our way through the bustling crowd of the Hanamikōji-dōri street, we cut through the grounds of the Yasaka-jinja shrine and entered Maruyama Park.

There wasn't a soul around. The drooping branches of the famous *shidarezakura* cherry trees, still wet from the rain, glowed in the light of the projectors illuminating them. We crossed the small arched stone bridge that stretched over the nearby circular pond and headed into the inner recesses of the park. It was extremely quiet. Even the sound of our footsteps on the gravel path was sucked into silence.

After we had progressed quite a bit, Kyōko asked in a low voice, "Say, where are we now?"

"Oh, I'm sorry. I forgot to explain where we are going. We're inside Maruyama Park."

We were on a slight incline, and Kyōko stopped in front of me.

"Is anybody around?" she whispered in my ear.

"No, no one in particular," I answered.

We exchanged a long kiss.

It occurred as naturally as the one at her house, but was incomparably more passionate. While we were kissing, it began to rain again. This made our kiss even more tempestuous. I pulled back an inch from Kyōko's lips and asked in a hoarse voice, "It's raining. Should I open the umbrella?" The most reasonable and silly question one could ever come up with.

"Who cares about the rain!"

She passionately sought my mouth again, and I returned her kiss with the same ardor. In no time, we were completely drenched. Shivering slightly, Kyōko leaned against me. Through the soaked, swelling frog on her chest, I could feel her breasts pressing against my chest. I had a very strong erection… which felt kind of nice in the early autumn rain.

My lips slowly slid down to the nape of her neck, and I gently nibbled her earlobes. Of their own accord, my hands slid between our bodies and cupped her breasts over the frog's bulging eyes. Her warm breath grazed my ear as she whispered, "Let's go home," in a strained voice.

At long last, I opened the umbrella, and we headed back the way we had come. Following a narrow path lined with lanterns, we entered the Yasaka-jinja shrine. There were many people enjoying an evening stroll in the precincts. They stared suspiciously, undoubtedly wondering why we were drenched like stray dogs even though we had an umbrella.

At the Higashiōji-dōri avenue, we hailed an MK taxi.

I hesitated for half a second, then said, "To Kurodani." As he drove, the driver kept glancing at us in the rearview mirror.

"Quite a downpour, huh? You'd better change those clothes quickly or you'll catch a really bad cold." He sounded like an old doctor making an unnecessary and obvious diagnosis.

Still drunk and in a state of ecstasy, Kyōko and I held hands. The seat cover was soon soaked from our clothes, but we couldn't care less. The streets of Kyōto whipped past at fantastic speed.

As we entered Kyōko's house, she took my hand and led me to a six-mat *tatami* room on the left, apparently her room. It was pitch dark, but Kyōko didn't turn on the lights.

"Wait here for a minute," she said, heading off somewhere.

I pulled the light's adjustment cord twice, and a soft orange radiance filled the small room.

Kyōko soon returned with two large towels. At home, she moved around absolutely freely without bumping into things. She sat down next to me, looking as if she had been exposed to a huge tidal wave. Her body was glowing, so beautiful and alluring I could hardly speak.

"Kyōko," I finally managed to whisper. "We'll catch cold if we stay like this."

"That's why I brought towels!" she announced proudly and began to take off her cardigan.

"Would you mind drying me off?" she asked, in the tone of voice used for buying a book of bus tickets.

She started peeling off her clothes, one layer at a time. I grabbed a towel and slowly began drying her hair. As I did so, she continued to undress. She didn't have much on to begin with, but it seemed to take an eternity. The room began to heat up. The next thing I knew, she was stretched out on the *tatami* absolutely naked—except for the gold necklace and earrings. "The Jewels," the title of a poem by Baudelaire, came to mind for an instant, but I was too overwhelmed to recall a single line.

Kyōko's breathing quickened. As I was drying her body, she reached for the buttons of my shirt.

"Let me dry you off, too."

The next moment, we were locked in a tight embrace. Then just like that, we made love on the *tatami*.

The fact that Kyōko wasn't a virgin both surprised me and brought me a particular sense of ease. When and with whom had she had physical relationships? This was a mystery, but her gasping, quivering, and intent pursuit of pleasure as she pressed my head to her breasts, made clear that she knew what she was doing. I was tempted to ask about the history behind these movements, but I didn't say anything. We became one in body and soul, and were soon drenched in sweat.

A little later, Kyōko nestled her face under my arm and gave a little sneeze. "Seems I've caught a cold," she said, with a childish chuckle.

"Let me put out the bedding."

Still naked, I opened the closet, pulled out a futon, and laid it out beside Kyōko. Using a push of the elbow, she moved onto the futon, then wrapped her slender arms around my neck and pulled me on top of her.

After we had made love again, I rolled off to the side with arms and legs stretched out on the *tatami*. The mats felt cool and pleasant. Not thinking of anything in particular, I stroked them with my fingertips. Unlike those in my boarding house, they were in perfect condition. This made me suddenly think of Steevie, and I had to laugh.

"What's wrong?" Kyōko asked, brushing her long hair back over the pillow with both hands.

"Kyōko, I'm really sorry," I said, beginning to pick up my scattered clothes. "But Steevie's probably pretty angry, so I think it'd be safer for me to go now." Once I was dressed, I whispered, "See you soon," and gave Kyōko a little kiss below the chin.

"Who's Steevie?" she asked in a groggy voice.

"I'll introduce you soon."

When I left the small house, it was nearly morning. Faint rays of light streamed through a gap in the clouds hanging over the Higashiyama mountains. My wet clothes clung to my body, but I didn't care. The early morning sky was crystal clear, as if hinting at the realization of innumerable possibilities. As I walked along, I recalled the events of the previous evening one after another. What a series of marvelous surprises it had been.

Gazing at the ridgeline of the Higashiyama mountains, I mused over what had happened and made my way home.

Midway through September, it began to feel somewhat like autumn. Together with the slow change of season, university life grew more hectic. In an attempt to lessen my workload, I read "The Cuckoo" to Kyōko. Towards the end of the story, when it became obvious that Takeo and Namiko would never meet again, Kyōko interrupted me.

"This guy really infuriates me."

"Wow, what's wrong?" I asked, lifting my head from the book in surprise.

"He doesn't even *try* to protect her. Neither from society, nor from his own mother. How can I put it? He doesn't resist in the slightest way. Don't you think that's pathetic? He shouldn't abandon his wife—no matter what other people think or say. He's a coward." She appeared seriously angry.

I smiled. "I understand what you're saying, but that's not how things were back then. No matter how much he loved her, he would need to have a lot of guts to go against everyone, to bring back a wife with tuberculosis."

Kyōko was silent.

"But you're right, it's rather ridiculous that he wouldn't even complain—even after his mother forced him to divorce." Though I had started off defending Takeo, I realized I wasn't convinced myself and had switched position in midstream.

The contradiction didn't escape Kyōko. "You wouldn't make a very good lawyer," she said, laughing.

"You're right. I'll never be a lawyer. And I'll probably never be a literary critic either."

Kyōko's mother must have noticed the change in our relationship, but she never said a word. Even when my visits to their house, now wrapped in ever deepening autumnal tints, became a daily occurrence, she never mentioned a thing. Quite the contrary, she always welcomed me with overwhelming kindness.

The three of us often ate together in the small living room facing the garden. For me, who had a hole in my stomach the size of Mt Fuji's crater because of all the unhealthy food at the school cafeteria and Sanpō Hanten, these healthy meals were a blessing. Sometimes we'd go to a fancy supermarket on the Shirakawa-dōri street—fancy by *my* standards of living anyway—and get the necessary ingredients for my specialty: Provence cuisine. However, making French cuisine using the chopsticks, knives, pots, and pans of a small kitchen designed exclusively for Japanese cooking wasn't easy. You really need the proper environment to do things properly.

On her first visit to my boarding house, Kyōko was endearingly moved when she met Steevie. By stroking his small head, long ears, and soft back, she acquired a thorough understanding of his appearance. During the procedure, Kyōko, Steevie, and I didn't make a sound, and the room was absolutely silent. Eventually, Kyōko put her hands back on her lap.

"He's a charming little fellow. I haven't petted a rabbit since elementary school, but I'm sure Steevie and I will become good friends. We understand each other." She looked exceedingly confident.

"It's a bit unusual for him to behave so well. He's usually really cautious with strangers. I guess he's got a crush on you."

"Do you think so?" said Kyōko with a smile. Then she petted him again.

In my small room on the second floor, we spent a lot of time talking and a lot of time making love. For me, having sex with Kyōko was a new and wonderful experience. She would begin by running her lips and fingertips over my entire body. This was like a ritual for her and took an extraordinary amount of time. Licking, smelling, nibbling, and touching, she explored every inch of my body over and over. Being touched and examined in such a way further aroused my desire.

When I couldn't bear the urge any more, Kyōko would gently take me into her arms. As we slowly reached orgasm together, her expression gradually changed like the autumn sky. At these moments, she looked ecstatically happy. Seeing her contentment made me genuinely happy, too. I felt as if my deepest needs were being fulfilled.

One evening, an earthquake struck while we were making love. We didn't notice at first, as it was difficult to distinguish our own movements from the shake of the quake. I was a bit scared when I realized what was happening.

"Hey, do you feel that? Isn't it a little dangerous?" I blurted out.

Kyōko paid no attention.

"Don't worry. Just ignore it," she sighed, as she hugged me even tighter. "Just go on riding the wave."

Just go on riding the wave! As we embraced again, I couldn't help thinking about what a neat expression that was. Before long, the earthquake was over, but in my body, the reverberations seemed to linger forever.

"In Japan, you don't often hear about people doing it when earthquakes hit, do you?" I asked.

"Well, I don't really know," she answered, as if she had not quite caught what I meant.

"Take Tōkyō, for instance. They've got a population of about thirteen million, right? Since the age of people having sex ranges from… let's be open-minded and say, fifteen or sixteen… to… oh, I don't know… I imagine people are still hanging in there at seventy. Making a rough estimate, that'd be about half the population, or at least six million people. If we then figure that about ten percent just happened to be involved in this intense physical activity—just like we were—that gives us about six hundred thousand. And that's just for Tōkyō. Considering the numbers, don't you think it's strange you hardly ever hear about this sort of thing?"

Kyōko burst out laughing.

"You come up with the strangest ideas." Her laughing on my chest tickled. "The numbers might work out that way, but I doubt there're many opportunities for bringing up such a topic in conversation."

After sex, Kyōko would explore my body once more with her fingers. But her touch was less sensual and seemed more aimed at remembering the shape of my face and body. Her hands moved gently, the fingertips just skimming over the surface or occasionally pressing down as if to measure the thickness of my shoulders or my chest.

Autumn passed quickly. It turned out to be the most beautiful autumn I spent in Japan—and also the last.

Kyōko and I boarded a city bus and set out along the meandering roads north to Ōhara. When we arrived at the Sanzen-in temple, we tried *shakyō*, copying sutras by hand. To tell the truth, this was no easy task. I let Kyōko hold the brush, and then took her hand lightly in mine. We wrote out the sutras one *kanji* ideogram after the other. This took a mind-boggling amount of time. The suspicious stares while we were engrossed in this heretical behavior only made matters worse.

When we finished, we linked arms and strolled through the temple grounds.

"I love walking with you like this," said Kyōko, clinging to my arm. "I'm sure that people don't even notice I can't see."

On sunny days, she playfully wore a gaudy pair of pink and orange sunglasses with a string around her neck. She looked great in them, and as long as she didn't do anything out of the ordinary, no one would ever guess she was blind. *Concealing* her disability became a kind of game. For instance, we'd have her carry a little camera, and then I'd say, "Just push the button," in a loud voice, and she'd take pictures to the sound of my voice. The developed photos turned out to be quite unique.

As we left the Sanzen-in temple, sunlight was cascading through the trees, an orange glimmer that fell on the bright red leaves covering the gravel path.

"Let me treat you to something special," I said, pulling Kyōko by the arm into the small fancy restaurant we were passing.

I chose the cheapest course on the menu of *kaiseki-ryōri*, the refined Japanese cuisine for which Kyōto was famous. Though I read the menu over and over, the ingredients of each individual dish remained a complete mystery. Having them explained just seemed too much trouble, so I had no alternative but to choose based on price. Even the cheapest course cost over fifteen hundred yen per person.

"Can a student afford to spend this kind of money?!" asked Kyōko with a look of amazement.

"No problem," I said, laughing her off. "My part-time job is starting tomorrow, so funds will begin pouring in soon."

A middle-aged woman in a kimono carried in the *kaiseki-ryōri* dishes on trays.

"There's not very much for fifteen thousand yen," I reported to Kyōko in a whisper.

We began eating, but this time, Kyōko's *cover* was completely blown. The food was difficult to eat even for someone who can see, and Kyōko had a really hard time. I explained the shape and position of the dishes one by one, and relying on that explanation, she carried the food to her mouth with her chopsticks. Considering the trouble we had to go through, the taste was nothing to write home about, and we both ended up rather disappointed.

When we reached Kurodani, the autumn sky was already dark, and stars were flickering overhead. As we stood on the dimly lit gravel path in front of her house, she tugged on my sleeve.

“Say, I’ve been meaning to tell you… during the summer, I spent some time looking for a job in Tōkyō. I’ve been enjoying a carefree lifestyle, and I don’t really need the money, but I can’t spend my whole life doing nothing, right? Pretty soon, I’ll have to decide on a career. I don’t have all that many options, but I figured I should start looking.”

The light scent of fragrant-olive trees drifted towards us on the evening wind.

“I’m not complaining, mind you. If I were willing to do the type of work that blind people are *expected* to do, there’d be plenty of opportunities. But I hate that kind of work. You know what I mean, right? I applied to many companies, but at the interview, they always ask: ‘Is commuting going to be okay?’ How do they suppose I attended school for fifteen years? Do they think my mother gave me a piggy back ride every day?”

I didn’t say anything.

“Anyway, yesterday I received an offer, and I wanted to tell you about it… I’m wondering what to do. I just can’t picture myself working in an office next spring. But then again, I still have some time to think about it.”

Before I could answer, she once more tugged on my sleeve, confirmed the location of my head with her right hand, and gave me a peck on the cheek. Watching her enter the house, I was extremely confused.

My job teaching English conversation started the following day. Standing in front of the whiteboard for the first time in a while, I experienced an indescribable sense of futility. A sensation I had forgotten since the beginning of fall—or to be more exact, since the day Kyōko and I kissed in Maruyama Park. I had convinced myself I was living in a pure “Japanese world” in my relationship with Kyōko, through my studies of Japanese literature, and even in my daily routine, so having to return to the shallow world of teaching English conversation was unbearable. For me, it was agony; I felt as if I were prostituting myself.

In the course of commuting to Ōsaka, however, this repulsion gradually waned, and I eventually stopped worrying about it.

When unpleasant experiences in my everyday life occasionally occurred, I became bitter and disillusioned. One incident took place when we were eating *tonkatsu* deep-fried pork cutlet in a restaurant called Yamamuraya. The place was famous for the stupendous size of its servings, so I had cut my midday classes and invited Kyōko to go with me.

As usual, I quickly read out the menu for Kyōko and then ordered for the two of us. Even though I was the one who had ordered—and this happened frequently when I was out with Japanese or Asian-looking friends as well—the guy turned to Kyōko, who is Japanese, and repeated my order. But Kyōko didn't realize she was being looked at. To help her out, I said, "*Hai, hirekatsu teishoku o futatsu kudasai.*" I guess he didn't think my Japanese was good enough because he replied in stilted, incoherent English, "Two, big Japanese pork, lunch, okay?" Refusing defeat, I repeated in my best Japanese, "*Sono tōri, hirekatsu teishoku o futatsu kudasai.*" I was getting pretty exasperated.

Thirty minutes later, two enormous pork cutlets were brought to us, but instead of the usual disposable *waribashi*, only forks and spoons were on our trays. Wondering if this particular restaurant didn't use chopsticks, I looked around at the other customers. Sure enough, everyone was eating their Frisbee-sized cutlets with standard *waribashi* chopsticks. Since that was the case, I wanted chopsticks, too. What's more, they'd be a lot easier to use for Kyōko.

When I politely asked, "*Sumimasen, o-hashi moraemasu ka?*" the guy yelled out with the same stupid English pronunciation as before, "Oh you Japanese, chopstick okay?" and slammed two pairs on our table as if it was the most cumbersome task.

That was just too much! I had never seen Kyōko look so depressed, and the other customers were also obviously ill at ease. Just as I was wondering how anyone could enjoy *tonkatsu* in such a place, Kyōko seemed to read my mind and whispered, "Let's get out of here." I paid the check and we left—leaving the grotesque pork cutlets untouched.

Some truly unique characters used the *sentō* near my boarding house. Sitting next to Kyōko on the veranda at her house, I told her about them. To start off, I described the middle-aged guy who owned a fish shop in the nearby shopping arcade. He started working at the crack of dawn, so he would have his wife run the shop in the afternoon. By six o'clock, he was usually at the bath.

"The guy's got the strangest quirk," I explained. "He never gets in the tub until just before closing time. Can you imagine? He comes at six, and stays until the very end. Then, with just ten minutes left, as if suddenly remembering something important, he literally dives in the tub."

"That'd be five or six hours, right? What does he do during all that time?" Kyōko's question hit the nail on the head.

"That's a good question. Actually, in his washbowl, he doesn't just carry soap and shampoo and other common things; he's got an old transistor radio. I mean real old, like what you'd find at a bargain sale in a pre-war factory, the kind you don't see any more. When he arrives at the *sentō*, he sits cross-legged with his back against the wall of the tub. Then he carefully spreads his small towel for *privacy* and places his washbowl with the antique radio between his legs." I explained as accurately as I could.

"And then?"

"And then? He listens to the radio, of course. He looks like he's in seventh heaven, what with his eyes closed and the volume turned up full blast. Usually he listens to baseball. So what do you think of that? Sitting stark naked in a warm place, listening to the ball game—pretty cool way to spend the evening, don't you think? I was quite impressed the first time I saw it."

"Yes, it doesn't sound bad at all," Kyōko laughed cheerfully.

"If that was the entire story, there'd be nothing to complain about, but there's more. If you spent every day handling fish, cutting fish, wrapping fish, and handing fish to customers, you'd smell pretty bad, no matter how clean you tried to stay. This guy is no exception. The stench is just unbelievable. It's a stench potent enough to make every fly in Japan want to evacuate and emigrate to a clean island in the south. What's more, he never washes before getting in the tub."

I paused.

"Regardless of when the ball game ends, that huge body of his, reeking of the sea, plunges in the tub at exactly the same time every day—just like a perfectly programmed time bomb. Of course, he only scrubs off afterwards."

"That's rather filthy," Kyōko said with a frown.

"Isn't it? That's why my top priority at the *sentō* is to get in the tub before he does."

"You do go through all kinds of hardships, don't you?" Kyōko teased me.

"By the way," I added. "According to my observations, people in Tōkyō and Kyōto seem to have very different ways of using the *sentō*."

"How is that?"

"In Tōkyō, for example, people wash from head to foot *before* getting in the tub. The idea is to warm your body in the shared tub after getting clean. In Kyōto, it's the opposite. People soak in the tub and wash *after* getting warm—just like the fish shop owner with the antique radio."

In Kyōto, I noticed something else: after getting undressed, men in Tōkyō paraded around naked without shame. But on the same island of Honshū, just a three-hour Shinkansen ride to the west, men did their utmost to hide themselves with their small washing towels, and would sooner die than expose anything.

I told Kyōko about this as we gazed at the garden adorned in its autumn colors. She showed a lot of interest. "That's an intriguing difference in behavior," she said, leaning her shoulder against mine. "So what do you do? Do you cover yourself?"

I chose not to answer.

She grew even more curious when I told her about the yakuza gangster covered with tattoos who was sitting next to me the previous day and also about an old man who had forgotten his dentures on the tile floor a few days before that.

"Say, I'd love to peep at that *sentō* of yours," she announced with a straight face.

I raised an eyebrow and looked at her.

"Well, I'd be happy to take you, but what will you do once you're there? I'd *love* to guide you in the women's section and give you a full account. Unfortunately, that's impossible."

But Kyōko wasn't one to give up easily. I ended up taking her to the public bathhouse one evening a few days later. The woman at the entrance watch stand looked a bit annoyed when I explained the situation, but she agreed to give Kyōko a helping hand.

After the bath, we walked arm in arm to the Shirakawa river. We strolled along next to the shallow current for a while, and then sat down on a narrow stone bridge. I opened a can of beer and handed it to Kyōko. She rotated the can slightly, located the mouth opening and took two big swallows with gusto. Then she rested her head on my shoulder and remained silent for quite some time.

I opened a can and drank some beer, too. Then I closed my eyes. Concentrating, I tried to get a grasp of my surroundings by relying on senses other than sight. But it didn't work out too well. I couldn't hear a thing apart from the faint sound of the flowing river and the laughter of kids playing in the neighborhood. The odd silence only made me feel nervous and want to open my eyes again.

But repressing that urge, I began to pick up new sensations. A scent of soap and shampoo wafted from Kyōko's body. For late October, it wasn't all that cold. I felt the relative warmth of the air on my skin, as if for the first time. Only the stone bridge under my hands felt surprisingly cold.

"They say Buddhist monks used to cross this narrow bridge during religious training," I said, breaking the silence but keeping my eyes closed. "That's why it's called *Gyōjabashi*."

"Is that right?" Kyōko said, not showing much interest in my display of superficial knowledge. "What I'm concerned about, is that it's going to rain soon."

"How would you know that?" I said, slightly annoyed.

"I just do," she said with confidence. "I can hear the wind rustling in the trees. And there's that distinctive smell that precedes rain in the air."

I opened my eyes and looked up at the twilight sky. Ominous rain clouds—just above the Chion-in temple—were silently moving in from beyond the Higashiyama mountains. Nearby, the drooping branches of the willows were gently swaying in the breeze. I only noticed these subtle signs, however, after straining my eyes and peering into the growing dimness around the river. I couldn't hold back a sigh. At such moments, I always felt torn between admiration and loneliness. Though Kyōko existed on the same physical plane, she experienced a completely different world—one that I could never share. Her capacity for getting at the essence of things was just too accurate, too sharp.

Soon, the wind grew stronger, and a soft pitter-patter of large raindrops began to fall on the surface of the river like warm tears tumbling down from the sky. I felt even more forlorn as I watched.

I was reading Kaikō Takeshi's *Natsu no Yami* (Darkness in Summer) aloud to Kyōko. The novel was full of very sensual passages, and as I continued reading, I couldn't help wondering why Kyōko always picked books with such *stimulating* effects. Midway through, she circled behind me and leaned against my back. I lifted my head up from the page for a second.

"Please go on," she said, in no more than a whisper. When she tossed her head back, I could feel her soft hair brushing against my neck. Imperceptibly, we slipped into the same titillating atmosphere as when I had been reading *Henry and June*. A warm sweetness enveloped me, and my throat became dry.

Kyōko's mother, who had been rummaging around in the next room doing housework, was suddenly standing in the doorway of the living room, listening. The weight of Kyōko against my back and her mother looking at me with a friendly twinkle in her eye made me feel all the more restless. The presence of these two women made me very self-conscious, and I realized how difficult it was to read aloud *while being watched.*

The next day we visited the Jun'ichirō Tanizaki Memorial Museum in Ashiya. A heavy rain had been falling all morning, but when we arrived at the museum, it was unbelievably sunny.

Against all expectations, the museum was an extremely modern building. As we walked around inside, I explained the various exhibits to Kyōko. We came up to a small *tatami* mat room with a wooden sign that read, "Tanizaki's Study." On the other side of the room, we could see a Japanese garden with a path circling a small pond. This was obviously a re-creation of one of the many studies of Tanizaki, a writer who was famous for moving frequently. Nonetheless, I felt I had caught a glimpse of the *authentic thing* I was always searching for in Kyōto. But I was incapable of expressing my feelings in words.

Another sign in front of the room explained that Tanizaki's everyday life was methodical in an almost fanatical way. As I read this out to Kyōko, a gray-haired man kept staring at us without the slightest regard for our feelings. We walked off to the next display. Later on, however, as I was explaining the exhibit of Tanizaki's modern translation of *Genji Monogatari* (The Tale of Genji), he reappeared and came up to us.

"Coming all the way from the United States to work as a volunteer. This is truly admirable!" he said, in the most impressed tone of voice.

"I'm not American, and this has nothing to do with volunteer work!" I answered in a huff.

Taken aback, he didn't say a word.

After we left the museum, Kyōko pulled my arm and whispered in my ear, "You shouldn't bully old men who are just trying to be friendly."

"I know. But people who jump to such simplistic conclusions really irritate me."

We walked in silence through a quiet residential area. As we were climbing a steep hill that ran alongside a stream, large clouds moved across the sky overhead, and I could catch glimpses of blue between them. The beautiful outline of Mt Rokkō off in the distance cheered me up again.

We paused when we reached the top of the hill.

"Is this sort of thing fun for you?" I asked, hesitantly bringing up a question that had been on my mind for quite some time. The moment I uttered it, I realized how extremely stupid a question it was and wished I could have taken it back immediately.

"What's that supposed to mean?" Kyōko asked in a shrill voice I had never heard before.

"Oh, there's no deep meaning. Just something I've sometimes wondered about."

"Does this have anything to do with the fact that I'm blind?" she asked, with even more tension in her voice.

"I can't explain exactly, and I'll probably be misunderstood. It's just that..." I couldn't find the proper words.

A heavy silence weighed on us for a while. The clouds moved across the sky from right to left.

"You are *so* stupid! I have always been blind. Even if I can't see you I enjoy being with you. Isn't that more than obvious? Your explanations are a pleasure, and they really help me understand my surroundings. Even if I'm blind, I love walking with you like this. For now, that's all that counts. So don't come up with such a stupid thing again. It really hurts my feelings." The expression on her face was one of anger and sadness.

Not knowing what to say, I mumbled a clumsy apology, but an awkward feeling had crept between us. Unable to dispel this uneasiness, we boarded the train and returned to Kyōto.

We barely exchanged a word during the entire trip.

Later at night, we made love in my small room and reconciled without further discussion.

The university presentations that were scheduled for me to give right after the summer break ended up being postponed to late October. In order to prepare for them, I cut classes and work, and locked myself up in my room to study.

My seminar presentation was carried out without too much trouble. I've never been good at speaking in front of people, but I received a relatively decent evaluation. Which is to say, I got a token comment from my professor, and no reaction from the other students. I spoke alone in the silent classroom, my classmates showing no interest whatsoever. The second the bell rang, they dashed out the door like mice from a sinking ship.

One student in my class was a girl named Koike. Whenever I caught a glimpse of her long, perfect, slender legs, I became light-headed and thought how lucky I was to be in this Seminar on Modern Literature.

On the other hand, her excessively attractive legs had a tantalizing power over all male students, and sitting across from her made it difficult to know where to look. For this reason, since our desks were arranged in a U-shape, I always was careful to *stay on her side*. But standing at the front of the classroom made it nearly impossible to avert my gaze from those elegant legs.

I certainly wasn't the only one fascinated by Koike's legs. Whenever my eyes *accidentally* turned in her direction, others were already staring, too. When I traced those stares back to their owners, I discovered that they belonged mostly to students, but also occasionally to the teacher. There's nothing wrong with a professor taking an interest in the unique geometry of a girl's legs, but meeting together on Koike's legs felt rather awkward.

Teaching English conversation was the same hollow ordeal as ever.

On the train home, with my head leaning against the cold windowpane, I stared blankly into the night. Flashes of artificial lights of some city shooting by alternated with the reflection of my own face, the train's interior bright behind me. When we flew past a station, the people standing on the platform vanished behind us in half a second—like the evil aliens of a science fiction movie being sucked into another dimension. I wasn't particularly interested in these things; I was just tired. I could hear neither the rattling of the train nor the conversation of the office ladies in front of me. I was lost in a comfortable, starry-eyed silence.

Racing through the darkness, I gradually regained a feeling of serenity. I only wished I could continue like this all the way to the Sea of Okhotsk. Unfortunately, one's personal desires and the business priorities of a train company run on separate tracks. The train stopped with distressing exactness at the appointed time and designated location in Sanjōkeihan station.

The Sanjō-dōri avenue was mobbed with businessmen heading home from work and other people hurrying to various destinations. A trolley clattered past in the direction of the Higashiōji-dōri avenue intersection.

When I reached Sanpō Hanten, the Chinese restaurant was hopelessly crowded. The only empty seat was at a table near the entrance. If I chose to sit there, I'd have the cold wind hitting me in the back every time someone entered or left, and I'd barely be able to see the small television at the opposite side of the room. On top of that, I'd have to share the table with somebody else. But I was starving, so I reluctantly took the seat.

For the first time in ages, I ordered an extra large *miso champon*, *gyōza* dumplings, and a beer. They brought me my drink right away, but I had to wait for the food. With so many customers, I could hardly complain.

I glanced at the TV. Four commercials were aired in a row: two for baby diapers and two for sanitary napkins. Why do they feed us this crap during mealtime? Exasperated, I turned away. Gazing at my mug, I heaved a little sigh. After some time, a couple of students stood up, paid their bill at the register, and left. As expected, the noise from the street swept in with a gust of cold wind.

I picked up my beer and moved to one of the vacated seats. The *miso champon* and *gyōza* were brought out seconds later. With heapings of shrimp, squid, and vegetables over perfectly cooked noodles in a richly flavored soup, the *champon* was exquisite. My soul was fulfilled and my heart leapt for joy. Smacking my lips, I reached out for a *gyōza* with my chopsticks. It melted in my mouth—as if it weren't even a *gyōza*. The delicious food made me sigh with contentment. I took another swig of beer.

After repeating the process two more times, I reached a state of satisfaction that I hadn't experienced for a long time. When I finished my *gyōza*, I poured the soy sauce, the *rāyu* orange chili oil, and the vinegar sauce from the *gyōza* plate over my noodles, making the flavor even stronger. After slurping up the final noodle and gulping down the last drop of soup, I was completely satiated. A little burp welled up from the pit of my stomach, and as I got another taste of the *miso* and other ingredients, I couldn't suppress a smile. I didn't feel like going home. My seat was comfortable, and I wanted to remain in this state of dazed ecstasy.

I took another glimpse at the TV. It was some kind of science fiction movie: I couldn't see too well, but a crowd was thronging in front of a massive wall, apparently the Berlin Wall. Young guys who had climbed on top were swinging sledgehammers to tear it down. The wall was so hard, however, that even the heaviest blows only sent a few chips of concrete flying.

I polished off the rest of my beer. Give me a break… a movie about tearing down the Berlin Wall. What's next? A film about the discovery of an iceberg on Mars and the Inuit settling in? Oh, well. Viewers always want something new, so movies might as well be imaginative and diverse.

When I glanced at the TV again, a crane was hoisting up a section of the wall. Another cheer rose from the crowd. Some people were drinking champagne.

I took a closer look.

I almost had a heart attack. The quality of the picture obviously wasn't that of a movie. The people in the crowd obviously weren't actors or extras. I got goose bumps, a shudder shook my body, and a shiver ran down my spine. This wasn't a movie; it was the news. People were actually tearing down the Berlin Wall. My hands trembling, I was on my feet before I even realized it.

I stood with my eyes glued to the set. I knew what I was watching was real, but I couldn't quite fathom what was happening. I felt a jumbled mix of joy and fear. The announcer's face appeared in the lower right hand corner, together with the caption, "Fall of the Berlin Wall, Democratization of Eastern Europe." In a stupor, I collapsed into my chair again. The empty porcelain bowl on my table struck me as being utterly void of meaning. For a while, I couldn't stop shaking. What a restricted and austere existence I had been leading. The historical fall of the Berlin Wall—through a chain of events I had completely ignored—was occurring before my very eyes. The realization that I'd been living in a dream, completely cut off from the real world, nearly threw me into a panic.

From within the small TV on the oily air conditioner unit, the world was calling me… For a split second, I heard the inviting clamor from the other side.

I gathered the empty beer mug, *gyōza* plate, and *champon* bowl into the center of the table, and slipped my used chopsticks back into their paper sheath. Then I paid my bill at the register and left. The chilly evening air was invigorating. I pulled up the collar of my leather jacket, shoved my hands into my pockets, and headed to my boarding house in silence—all the while thinking about the crowd ten thousand kilometers away.

Several days later, Kyōko and I were walking up the steep stone steps of the Kibune-jinja shrine, north of Kyōto, in a cold drizzle. Red *tōrō* lanterns lined each side of the stairway. As always, I described our surroundings and guided Kyōko's hand to the wet moss, the massive tree trunks, the stones, and whatever else she wished to touch.

At a kind of viewing platform, we sat down on a bench. Under the same umbrella, we ate the *yakiniku* lunch that Kyōko had prepared. The arrangement of grilled meat and vegetables reminded me of an abstract modernist painting, but it tasted delicious.

On the train home, Kyōko fell asleep as we were heading towards Demachi-Yanagi, the terminal in Kyōto. I gazed at her sleeping face. I wasn't thinking of anything particular, when suddenly, it dawned on me why I always felt so at peace with her.

If you thought about it, the explanation was very simple, but it was precisely because it was, that it hadn't occurred to me for a long time.

She couldn't see me.

People in Kyōto always stared at me. Their behavior towards someone was always determined by outward appearances, which always made me feel uncomfortable. This is more or less what people do in all countries, but in Kyōto things were somewhat different. The process whereby they looked at someone and based solely on appearance instantly decided something about that person, totally ignoring his or her feelings—to a degree you couldn't help but admire—was absolutely unique.

This wasn't a simple matter that could be explained with common words such as "discrimination" or "close-mindedness." There was a subtle distinction-making mechanism, which at first seemed palpable, but turned out to be invisible and rather creepy. Even if you could feel the mechanism at work *physically*, it had no clear shape. Whenever I had tried to confront the problem, I had found myself eluded by something I couldn't define. There was no sound, clash, or pain in the confrontation, but its sheer repetition beat me up both physically and mentally.

And obviously, the source of all this was outward appearances. I guess I was exhausted from always being stared at. I was sick of having to play the role of the *gaijin* buffoon.

When I was with Kyōko, however, this naturally never occurred. Needless to say, for her outward appearances didn't exist. From the beginning, our relationship was based on voice, touch, and language—things that bound us *beyond* outward appearances.

Even if I made a mistake or used an inappropriate turn of phrase, Kyōko focused on the content of what I was trying to communicate. She had transcended nationality and race, and always interacted with me as a fellow human being. That's how I felt. If Kyōko could see me, our relationship would probably be completely different.

Knowing there was one person in this city that couldn't see me and could behave in a natural way brought me great peace of mind—more than I could ever express in words. I considered mentioning this to Kyōko, but I feared it might cause some misunderstanding, so I didn't.

She continued sleeping soundly until the small train reached the final station.

CHAPTER THREE

The year's end brought a series of unforeseen events, and something strange occurred just as I was about to concentrate on writing my graduation thesis. Within the span of one evening, I was dragged into something totally unexpected—the world of a small yakuza gang.

It all started with a single message left on my answering machine. When I returned to the boarding house, the phone's lamp was flashing like a heart rate monitor. I pushed the play button and an artificial metallic voice announced, "You have one message." Then the tape began to play.

A French-speaking male voice filled the room.

"Hello. My name is Jean Sallislaff. I'm a shoot director with French national television. I heard about you from Endō-*san* in Paris. We're about to start filming a documentary here, and the person scheduled to work as our interpreter and go-between fell ill. To make a long story short, we're in a real fix."

There was a pause. The man was choosing his words carefully. He spoke with perfect calm and composure.

"I work in collaboration with Endō-*san*, so I gave her a call in Paris, and she recommended you right off. We're staying at the New Miyako Hotel. Give me a call before the day is out. My number is—" At this point, the voice cut off, the recording capacity having been exceeded. I pushed the delete button, lit myself a Shinsei cigarette, and recalled my time in Paris.

I had met Endō-*san* quite by accident about five years ago. I was spending the summer in Paris, just before I started my job working on a ship. I was renting a small loft, which served as my base for wandering the streets of the city.

On that particular day, I was taking a stroll along the Seine. The wind was strong, and small brown-tinged waves rippled across the surface. Several barges, swaying with the current, were anchored along both banks. I heard a voice behind me. When I turned around, I saw a woman squatting on the embankment overlooking the river. She was unmistakably Asian, but I figured I should start off speaking in French.

"Something wrong?" I asked.

She turned around, slightly surprised.

"My cat disappeared a couple of days ago, and I've been looking for him ever since. I finally found him on that boat. I don't know how he got there, but it's too far from the bank for me to leap over, and he refuses to jump off. To make matters worse, the owner of the boat seems to be away."

She looked Japanese but spoke fluent French without a trace of an accent. Judging from her clothes and demeanor, she wasn't one of those Japanese tourists visiting Paris on holiday. She appeared to be in her mid-thirties and was quite attractive. When she spoke, she gazed at me with kind eyes, which had small charming wrinkles in the corners.

The cat on the boat suddenly appeared. It was a red-haired monstrosity.

"The boat's moving back and forth pretty regularly," I said, as if to myself. "If I time my jump properly, I should be able to get on board easily."

She stared up at me in complete awe. I was much younger in those days, and I couldn't resist that kind of glance. The large hull was just then moving to shore. I waited for the right moment and leapt across. From behind, I heard the woman's cry of admiration and a smattering of applause.

I had boarded all right, but the cat was nowhere to be seen. On the boat, the stench of the Seine was more oppressive, and the wind felt stronger. I spotted two pointy triangular ears behind a pile of rope. It eventually took me half an hour to tackle that cat. Aiming towards the woman on shore, I tossed it over like a rugby ball. The cat gave a startled squeal but landed dexterously on all fours and dashed to the woman. Cradling it happily in her arms, she nuzzled her cheek against its face. What a melodramatic display!

The accident happened when I tried to return to shore.

After a moment of hesitation, I made my move for another big jump. But my right foot slipped on the wet deck, and a second later, I was plunging head first into the Seine. Although it was summer, the water was so cold I thought I was going to have a heart attack. And the smell was absolutely revolting. Overcome by the sense of having fallen into some terrifyingly unsanitary substance, I was on the verge of panic. I somehow made it back to shore, but my swimming was completely pathetic.

Dripping foul-smelling water and sludge, I stood in front of the Japanese woman. "You can't fully appreciate how bad the Seine smells until you've actually fallen in."

She laughed and thanked me for rescuing her cat.

We scurried to her apartment nearby, where I took a hot shower. While I waited—clad in one of her silk gowns—for my washed clothes to dry, we chatted over tea in her stylish living room.

She told me she'd been living in Paris since she was eighteen, that she'd received a master's and doctorate in art history from the Sorbonne, and that she was now working as a coordinator for various art and culture exchanges between France and Japan.

After this rather uncommon first meeting, we spent much of the rest of the summer chatting together over cheap rosé at a small restaurant on the hill of Montmartre.

Lost in these reminiscences, I stood up. The room was filled with cigarette smoke, so I opened the window to let in some fresh air.

Hearing about Endō-*san* after all these years was unexpected enough, but the content of the phone message was even more intriguing. I decided to call the New Miyako for more information. I was connected to Jean Sallislaff's room, and a man with the same voice as the one on my answering machine answered.

"I'll be having dinner at the French restaurant here at the hotel. Why don't you come and join me? I'll fill you in on the details then."

For a poor student accustomed to Sunday dinners at Sanpō Hanten and other cheap restaurants, the temptation of a French meal at the New Miyako was irresistible. Twenty minutes later, I was exchanging a firm and friendly handshake with Jean Sallislaff in the hotel lobby.

After we moved to the restaurant and ordered our meals, I observed him more closely. On the phone, he had sounded like the stereotypical TV director: cool, self-confident, and clever. Meeting him in person, however, conveyed a completely different impression. Though he appeared to be about forty, he had a babyish face, a receding hairline, and a gaze of child-like innocence that peeped from behind his glasses. He had the kind of face that conveys a favorable impression and immediately sets people at ease.

Another distinguishing feature was that he was fat. Now I don't mean just a little overweight. He looked more like a huge roly-poly *daruma* doll than a human being. Yet he seemed to be bursting with energy and looked pleasing to the eye. He was living proof that some people can be overweight yet manage to stay healthy.

He started filling me in on the project. At first, he spoke with restraint, but then he became more and more animated. Before I knew it, I was completely caught up in his explanation. The spectacle of a man with such a face and body speaking with such eloquence and enthusiasm had a powerful, magnetic appeal. He managed to get me really worked up in the most efficient way.

By the time dinner was over, I was seriously contemplating throwing myself into the project—while nevertheless worrying a little about what would happen with my thesis if I did.

Kyōko got all excited when she heard about the yakuza.

"It all sounds fascinating," she said. "You simply *must* do it. I understand your concern about your thesis, but I'm convinced that a break from the world of books will do you good."

Kyōko's mother, who was having tea with us, was equally enthusiastic.

"It's like becoming a character in a movie, isn't it? I've always wondered about the yakuza. I'm curious to know about what lies behind the façade. When the filming's finished, you'll have to tell us all about it. I'm looking forward to hearing about your adventures."

What a pair! Taken aback as much by the mother as by the daughter, I glanced outside. Most of the greenery in the garden was gone. The denuded trees stood in lonely rows on the slope behind the house.

I wanted to speak more in depth with Kyōko about my feelings, but I couldn't do so in front of her mother. I only managed to ask if she'd be willing to take care of Steevie while I was working on the yakuza project.

"Sure, I'd love to. My mother will handle cleaning his box, while I take care of feeding him and showering him with affection."

Over the next several weeks, I was to be dragged deeper and deeper into the closed and tumultuous world of the Japanese mafia.

Snow was gently falling when I arrived at the Ōsaka headquarters of the Kaizuka-*gumi* clan with the film crew. The building looked like any ordinary three-story apartment building, except that at the entrance was a double-paned glass barrier, with "Kaizuka-*gumi* Headquarters" written in impressive gold lettering. Behind the glass was a huge *real* stuffed lion and security cameras mounted on both sides.

"The cameras are for protection against attacks," Kaizuka-*oyabun*, the clan chief, explained. "The lion's a thank-you gift from another *oyabun* for a little job we did." Some people do come up with rather eccentric ideas for presents, I thought.

In the middle of the fluffy white carpet in the *oyabun*'s hideout was a large, low table partly surrounded by an L-shaped sofa that could seat about ten people. On the shelves surrounding us was an array of photographs, boxing trophies, Japanese swords, and other decorations. Taking a closer look at the pictures, I noticed they showed Kaizuka-*oyabun* with various men, probably other mob bosses, in traditional *haori* half-length coats and *hakama* pleated skirts. In others, he was standing with famous sumō wrestlers and local politicians.

"I'm a Kyūshū man."

Leaning back in his leather chair, Kaizuka-*oyabun* finally started opening up to us on the second evening. Just out of the bath, he wore a white terry cloth robe, the tattoos on his chest visible between the folds of his collar.

"I was nine when they kicked me out of school. I don't remember what happened precisely, but I was returnin' some scissors to my teacher. I screwed up and handed 'em with the blade pointin' out. When she came to grab 'em, for some reason I pulled my hand back too fast. She only got a cut on her palm, but I was expelled right away. In a country school after the war, it was real easy to kick out some pain-in-the-ass kid."

The *oyabun* told us his story in a calm and quiet voice.

"I didn't dare go back home right away. I goofed off in town for a while, and after it got dark, I took my time walking home through the fields. I was dead scared of my old man. Sure enough, he went completely nuts. I barely got through the door when he nailed me with a punch that laid me out cold. When I came to, I was locked up in the closet, wrapped in a futon and tied up with my old man's belt. I was really terrified. It was pitch-black. I couldn't move, and I could hardly breathe. It was a real long night, and I pissed in my pants several times. In the morning, my sister untied me. She spoke real fast, warning me, 'If ya stay, he's gonna kill ya, so ya better make a run for it.' And that's how I ended up runnin' away from home. I never saw my old man or my sister again."

His eyes were glued on me as he spoke. I couldn't help detecting something unexpectedly fascinating and intelligent in that gaze.

"I left town, and for three years lived like a stray dog, stealin' food and wanderin' from place to place. I soon realized that becoming a yakuza was my only way to survive. I spent my teenage years movin' from gang to gang. I was sent to reform school three times. I spent most of my adult life in jail. I was sentenced three times: once for five years and seven months, another for two years and nine months, and the last for eight years and four months. The first two sentences I was takin' the rap for guys in my gang. The last one was for somethin' I actually did myself."

He smiled wryly and paused before continuing.

"In jail, I made friends with all kinds of guys, and when I got out, I figured I'd start my own gang. Guys I met during my days in prison just flocked to me. That's how the Kaizuka-*gumi* got started."

The gang's *wakagashira*, young chief-to-be, was sitting behind a huge desk counting a thick wad of ten-thousand-yen bills. Sometimes he'd stop counting and, with a blank expression, rub the back of his shaved head. On the wall behind him was an organizational chart, with nameplates arranged in five or six ranks. Names written in red were scattered amongst those in black.

"The red ones are guys in jail," Kaizuka-*oyabun* explained to us the next day.

One wall of the office was lined with a row of paper lanterns on which were written "Kaizuka-*gumi*." The room's most distinctive characteristic, however, was a TV of mind-boggling size. On top of the TV was a huge elephant tusk, sandwiched between the monitors for the two surveillance cameras. I had never seen such an immense television. It was so gigantic it could have served as a movie theatre for the elderly folks in the neighborhood. But then again, they probably wouldn't have liked what was playing on the extra-large screen: around-the-clock videos of yakuza films. The gang members sat glued in front of the TV all day long. Smoking cigarettes, squinting at the screen, licking and biting their chapped lips, they were completely engrossed in those movies.

We were finally allowed to film on the morning of our fourth day with the gang. Jean Sallislaff, who until then had been about as active as a bear in hibernation, awoke to his original lively self and began giving crisp and speedy orders. A light snow was falling, and as we were filming the building's exterior, Jean held out both hands—like an innocent child enjoying snowflakes tickling his palms.

"Well, time for golf practice," said the *oyabun*, waving us up to the roof. "You might want to film this as well."

On the roof was a small driving range. Far from the ledge and invisible from the street, the range was surrounded on four sides by high green netting. Kaizuka-*oyabun*, wearing gold-rimmed sunglasses (which he wore wherever he went, regardless of the weather), practiced his swing inside the enclosed area. After he hit a ball, one of his henchmen replaced it immediately, and he took another swing. I don't know much about golf, but he had a pretty strong and flexible swing. Quick as lightning, one ball after another went smashing into the net ten meters away. A large cemetery was visible in the distance, and for over an hour, the *oyabun* stood in the fluttering snow and sent golf balls flying towards the rows of gravestones.

"We've got a few guys buried there," he said after practice, as he wiped the sweat from his face with a towel handed to him by another henchman.

"In our line of work, you never know when you're gonna go," he continued as he handed off his club. "That's why we're always ready. Even so, there's no dying in vain. That's a credo of ours. It's hard to explain what that means exactly, but basically it's gettin' killed over some petty personal trouble you caused yourself. If it's for the gang, we're prepared to die any time."

That evening, we set off with the gang for Dōtonbori, an Ōsaka pleasure district. The gangsters squeezed into five Mercedes-Benzes, and we followed in our truck, which was loaded with equipment. Their driving was the most reckless I'd ever seen. Always keeping the *oyabun*'s white Mercedes-Benz surrounded by the other four black ones, they raced through the slushy streets at breakneck speed. To stay in formation, they had to be extremely aggressive; they ran stoplights, cut off other drivers, slammed their brakes at random, and ignored every traffic rule in the book.

Matsutani-*san*, our cameraman, filmed this wild car chase with his head sticking out through the sunroof. Cold air and snow streamed into the truck through the opening. Yes, it was like being in an action scene of a movie. I recalled Kyōko's mother's words and smiled.

In Dōtonbori, our first stop was a *yakiniku* restaurant. Being the interpreter, I was seated directly across from Kaizuka-*oyabun*. As he laid slices of meat on the grate with his chopsticks, he struck up a conversation with me.

"What're ya studyin' at that university in Kyōto?"

"Literature. Especially modern literature," I answered with a straight face.

"You mean Japanese literature?" he asked, as he checked on the grilling meat.

I nodded.

"Literature isn't somethin' one studies in college, is it? During all my time in prison, I read a truckload of books, but I don't remember ever readin' anythin' written by someone who studied literature in college. If you want to study literature, you've got to be willing to look at different sides of life and society to confront the ugly aspects of mankind. Stare them straight in the face. 'Cause it's only by knowing the dark side, that you'll see the real beauty in things." Chewing his meat slowly as he spoke, the *oyabun* stared straight at me.

We moved to a nightclub. When we entered, there were about ten women dancing on stage. They were topless, with breasts of various shapes and sizes swaying in rhythm to the music. We were led to a long narrow table to the left of the stage, and several women joined our group. I took a sip of whisky and started to chat with the girl who had snuggled up against me like a pet. But she didn't understand Japanese.

"There's two reasons why we go to places run by Koreans," one of the gang members told me. "The main one's that we're not welcomed very cordially by the Japanese. We pay our tab just like everybody else, but we ain't ever treated like real customers. The other reason is communication. These girls workin' here—as you just noticed—ain't too good in Japanese, so there's hardly no chance they'll grasp the details of what we're talkin' 'bout, which suits us just fine."

We filmed at the club for about an hour. The naked girls on stage put on quite an impressive show. Kaizuka-*oyabun*, wearing his dark, gold-rimmed glasses as usual, sipped his *mizuwari* water and whisky on the rocks. He didn't speak to anyone for nearly an hour. Then suddenly—without any warning—he stood up and said, "We're moving to the next place." Then he headed to the exit, and everyone hustled after him.

At the karaoke bar, we again sat at one table. A huge guy who bore a disturbing resemblance to a gorilla sat next to me.

The first one to sing was the *wakagashira* with the shaved head. Judging from his goofy self-absorbed expression, he was certainly doing his best, but he was an unbelievably horrible singer. He wasn't just tone-deaf. He was too loud and completely lacked any sense of rhythm. One of the women, unable to bear the sight of a customer making a spectacle of himself, picked up the other mike to help him get back on track, but he waved her off and went on singing by himself. This hellish cacophony went on for an hour and a half.

During all this time, my friendly neighbor the gorilla chattered away. A former professional wrestling champion, he now worked as a yakuza bodyguard. He joined Kaizuka-*gumi* because he admired the *oyabun*, and confided to me that he was "always ready to die for him."

I sipped my whisky and nodded appropriately. During his confession, however, he got worked up and started punching himself in the face.

"Check it out! Pretty cool, huh? You could punch me a billion times, and I'd never go down. In my pro wrestler days, guys'd pound and pound on me, but I'd never get knocked out. Go ahead! Punch me and see!"

He grabbed my hand and tried to force me to throw a punch, but I politely declined, saying, "I'll give it a try some other time."

A single punch of his looked strong enough to floor an ox, but he went on pummeling himself as if he were immune to pain. It pained me to watch, and I began to feel dizzy. Unable to bear it any longer, I downed the rest of my whisky in one gulp.

Shortly past three in the morning, we left. The drive home was another car race. All the swerving made me nauseous. The topless women dancers, the gangster harping about not being cordially welcomed, the imbecilic expression of the gorilla punching himself in the face without mercy—one after another, these images swirled around in my head. As they did, the *wakagashira*'s song dragged on in the background like an endless incantation.

We got to see a tattooing session. A white futon was laid out in the middle of a spacious ten-mat room, which had a huge mirror on the ceiling. A small machine was laid out on traditional Japanese paper covered with designs that reminded me of colorful *ukiyo-e*, woodblock prints of the floating-world. To the side were tiny white ceramic bowls filled with various dyes.

When I entered, a man in his fifties was sitting in *seiza* posture and putting all these items in order. Actually, I'd seen the guy visiting the gang's headquarters nearly every day. But he always went straight up to the second floor, and after several hours, left without exchanging a word with anyone. His presence was a complete enigma.

Like most of the gang members, his pinkies on both hands were short of a knuckle or two. It was his face that set him apart: he had bizarrely thick eyebrows that stretched into a perfectly straight horizontal line. It looked as if someone had taken a ruler and drawn a thick line over his real eyebrows with a magic marker.

That day, when we went to film the *wakagashira*'s getting tattooed, I learned that this mysterious fellow was the gang's tattooist and that his weird looking eyebrows were in fact tattoos.

“More than anything else, a tattoo’s a kind of trial for testin’ your courage in the face of pain, for seein’ how much you can endure,” he explained as he moved behind the futon and lined up the small ceramic cups. “That’s why long ago people called tattoos ‘etchings of endurance.’” When everything was ready, he plugged in the cord of a curious-looking device.

The *wakagashira* entered the room wearing nothing but a white loincloth. With the exception of his face, neck, hands, and feet, he was covered from head to toe with brightly colored tattoos. He bowed slightly to the tattooist and lay face up on the futon.

The tattooist took the mysterious instrument in his hand and showed it to us. “Long ago, people used the *tebori* tattooin’ method, usin’ needles attached to a bamboo stick. I invented this electric tool about ten, fifteen years ago. The needles are attached to the tip which moves like a sewin’ machine.” Holding the instrument in his right hand, he laid his left hand on the *wakagashira*’s chest. Like a doctor examining a patient, he silently inspected his work on the young man’s body.

Everything remained totally still for a while. Finally, the tattooist picked up what seemed to be a dirty towel in his left hand, applied color to the tip of the instrument, and switched on the machine. The noise of the small engine broke the silence. It was a peculiar humming metallic sound. Then he began tattooing the *wakagashira*’s chest.

“What I’m doin’ now is colorin’ a design I previously outlined in black ink. I basically use fourteen colors, but it’s the skin that makes the real difference. That’s the trickiest thing about tattooin’. Even if ya use the same color, dependin’ on the person’s condition on that particular day, when the punctures heal, ya gonna get subtle differences. So ya gotta check out the client closely, and if he’s got a slight fever, ya gotta use a lighter color, or if he’s tired, a slightly darker one. Ya gotta always be considerin’ stuff like that.”

He explained all this as if we were recording a program on tattooing for NHK’s Educational Channel. As he spoke, he never once lifted his head, fully concentrated on filling in the petals on his client’s chest. Every once in a while, he would raise his right hand, switch off the machine, and use the dirty towel he held in his left hand to wipe away drops of blood oozing from beneath the dye.

Breathing quietly, the *wakagashira* gazed at his image in the mirror on the ceiling. The hand filling in the petals moved up and down in rhythm with his breathing. Barely batting an eye, the *wakagashira* stared fixedly at his reflection in the mirror. His expression was markedly different from the silly look he had when singing karaoke. He must have been enduring a significant amount of pain, but he didn't even flinch.

When the session was over, he stood up as if nothing had happened, bowed in silence to the tattooist, and left the room. After the film staff had put away their equipment and left, I stayed behind to have a chat with the tattooist. He pulled out a stack of designs drawn in black ink on Japanese paper and laid a bunch of them on the futon. They included tigers, serpents, peonies, dragons, and samurai.

"Does tattooing really hurt that much?" I asked without giving it a second thought.

The tattooist didn't answer. With incredible speed, he grabbed my right hand and brought the electric instrument over it. I tried to pull back, but he held my hand pinned down with astonishing force.

"Don't worry. I didn't put no dye on, so it won't be a tattoo. Just a little scratch that'll heal in two or three days." He turned on the switch, and the droning of the machine filled the room again.

He worked on the base of my thumb for about a minute. The needles, moving at a dizzying speed, penetrated my flesh. I stared as if possessed. Little drops of blood occasionally dribbled from the wounds, but it wasn't as painful as I had expected. After a while, he turned off the machine.

"I thought it'd hurt more," I said.

He smiled. "That's 'cause you're all tensed up. And 'cause we only did it for a minute. It usually takes hundreds of hours to complete a tattoo, ya know. Some guys come to me every day for one or two years. Endurin' that kind of pain is in a whole 'nother category. By the way, your hand's gonna start stingin' in about thirty minutes. That's perfectly normal, so don't worry about it. In other words, the real pain comes after the tattooin' is finished."

He stood up.

"Well, I got another job, so I'm gonna get goin'. If ya ever wanna tattoo, gimme a call." He handed me his business card and left.

Sitting on the tatami with my legs crossed, I became lost in thought. The room was very quiet. I looked again at the white futon, the unfolded stacks of designs, the electric tool, and the small white containers of dye. Even with this evidence spread out before me, all that I had just witnessed—the tattooist with the black eyebrows, the *wakagashira* with the *jigoku-e* Scene of Hell drawing covering his entire body, and the device drilling holes in my hand—seemed like a faraway dream.

I glanced at the ceiling. The mirror looked down over the room from the same position as before. Reflected there, however, was no longer the *wakagashira*—but an unshaven Westerner. It took me a minute before I realized who it was.

As I gazed at my reflection in the mirror, I became aware of something: since my arrival, the gang members had never treated me like a foreigner. When they met someone, they put you in one of two categories: *friend* or *foe*. In order to gain their trust, we had to spend many late nights drinking, smoking, and talking with them. But even during those long hours together, they never showed any signs of making a distinction between Japanese and foreigners. At the same time, I never received that *strange foreigner* treatment reserved for foreigners who can speak Japanese. Such distinctions just weren't important to them. That's all there was to it.

Unlike the peculiar atmosphere of Kyōto, which always made me self-conscious of being a foreigner, the yakuza attitude put me at ease. Immersing myself in their world, I had been able to forget the issue entirely. Come to think of it, I had even completely forgotten what I looked like. That's why I was so surprised to see myself in the mirror on the ceiling.

I picked up the stack of designs and looked them over one by one. I realized that I had been holding back a lot of anger and grief, with which I was at a loss. I started to feel very restless. A dark bitterness welled up from the pit of my stomach. It took considerable time to ascertain the source of this unarticulated discomfort.

I recalled the many trivial yet indescribably disagreeable experiences that had pricked my soul like thorns. Until then, I hadn't been that conscious of them, but when I saw myself in the mirror, vivid memories came crashing down upon me like shards of glass.

People making distinctions based on outward appearances. Annoying students on their field trips. Idiotic businessmen. The drunkard concerned about where Japan was heading. Pretentious Japanese *kaiseki* cuisine. The *tonkatsu* shop owner. Innumerable suspicious glances. An endless series of slights.

Though all of this was no more than an accumulation of rather insignificant incidents, as I sat in the tattoo room, I realized that my tolerance to endure such matters had eroded.

I put the sketches back on the futon. The room remained silent. My right hand began to sting, just as the tattooist had predicted. This didn't bother me in the least. I agonized over what to do: I was dying to see Kyōko, but I never wanted to go back to Kyōto again.

CHAPTER FOUR

I ended up returning to Kyōto a few days later. Jean Sallislaff had asked me to come with the crew to Kyūshū to cover another yakuza gang, but I just couldn't put off my graduation thesis any longer. So I decided to head back.

I wanted to see Kyōko.

On the last day at Kaizuka-*gumi*, the gang members woke up early, lined the street in front of the building with oil drums, and lit bonfires inside them. Wearing nothing but a white *fundoshi* loincloth and a *hachimaki* headband, the men gathered for a *mochizuki-taikai*, a convivial communal event in which glutinous rice is pounded into soft cakes. When I parted from the clan, no one came to see me off, and no special words of farewell were spoken. Family members were also participating in the gathering, but all I got was a couple of rice-cakes handed over by the children. I slung my knapsack over my shoulder and walked to the nearest subway station.

The subway wasn't particularly crowded. After a short time, I got the feeling that something was out of kilter with my fellow passengers. It was like the first time I had used a Japanese-style toilet and wasn't sure in which direction to squat or how far to pull down my pants. The swaying businessmen wore similar trench coats and similar suits of similarly muted tones, and they read their *manga* and sports newspapers all bearing a similar expression. High school girls wearing navy blue uniforms and Burberry scarves chattered away like typical high school girls—starting their day in the same usual way.

And everyone had a full complement of fingers. It didn't register immediately, but this exceedingly unexceptional fact was what threw me off.

Without realizing it, I had grown completely accustomed to the gang members' all having shortened or missing fingers. Consequently, as I gazed at the passengers on the subway, I was surprised by all the *extra* digits. Our perception of what is normal, I guess, is like a highly adaptable animal, an intriguing creature with infinite possibilities, continually evolving to conform to its environment.

The room I returned to after my long absence was freezing. It reminded me of a slab of marble that had been sitting in a tuna freezer for a year. I felt like I had wandered into the wrong room by mistake, and it took me a while to unwind. With the room temperature lower than the temperature outside, it was difficult to enjoy a feeling of having *returned home*. The answering machine lamp was flashing like crazy, but I pushed the delete button instead of listening to the messages. I switched on the heater for the *kotatsu* and snuggled under the quilt cover.

With the telephone cord stretched to the limit, I dialed Kyōko's number from my seat under the *kotatsu*. She answered right away.

"So you're still alive," she said in a reproachful tone of voice. "We haven't heard from you in ages. We've been worried about you."

"I'm really sorry, but things were just crazy. I was so busy, time flew by before I knew it. It was like living on another planet."

She sighed.

"I guess that's a valid excuse. At any rate, I'm glad to hear you're okay."

I didn't say anything.

"So how was your little escape from the world of books?" she asked in a teasing tone.

"Well, not too bad," I answered meekly. "A lot of things happened, and I've learned a lot. Nothing deeply moving or outrageously impressive, but it was a really valuable experience."

There was a short silence.

"So, what are your plans for New Year's?"

"I just got back. I haven't really thought about it."

"Why don't you pass by and tell us about the filming over some *nishime*?"

"*Nishime*?"

"In Kansai, that's what we call the New Year's *o-sechi* dishes."

"Is that right? Well, okay. As long as I can finish a report which I have to hand in early next year. I was hoping to knock it out on New Year's Eve, so if it's not too much trouble, I'll see you early on New Year's Day."

Talking to Kyōko after so long somehow made me very cheerful.

"Don't be silly! It's no trouble at all," she said happily. "I'm sure my mother's looking forward to seeing you, too."

"Well, then… I look forward to seeing you." I wanted to say more, but I couldn't find the right words.

"*Well, I look forward to seeing you, too,*" Kyōko answered and hung up.

With a smile on my face, I got up from the *kotatsu* and replaced the receiver.

I changed into attire warm enough to survive an Antarctic winter and went downstairs. The kitchen was chilly. The other students had apparently gone home, and the house was eerily silent. I flipped through the stack of mail on top of the old refrigerator, but there was nothing addressed to me. I had completely forgotten the outside world over the past several weeks, and the outside world had completely forgotten me—that's often characteristic of our relationship.

The boarding house struck me as being even dirtier than usual. Unwanted old furniture had been abandoned in the inner courtyard, which we used for hanging our laundry, and the wild grass had grown so high that the ground was no longer visible. In the kitchen there were stacks of dirty dishes adorned with unidentifiable leftovers, and the Japanese-style toilet was literally covered with shit. As I passed through the kitchen, toilet, courtyard, and other rooms on the ground floor, I discovered all kinds of alien substances and was sickened by various potent smells.

Thoroughly disgusted, I began a major *ō-sōji* year-end household cleaning.

I gathered the discarded furniture into a corner of the yard and cut the grass with a rusty old kitchen knife. Cutting grass with an old rusty kitchen knife, just in case you've never tried, is a backbreaking task. When I finished these chores, I bagged up the garbage artistically scattered through the house, washed the dishes, and hosed down the toilet with copious amounts of water. Why Japanese guys would cheerfully continue using such a toilet day after day, and rather die than clean it, was for me one of the greatest mysteries of the Orient.

Lastly, I threw the clothes I had worn during the yakuza project into the wash. The old washing machine made a dreadful rattling noise during the spinning cycle. It sounded as if firewood had been tossed in by mistake.

After hanging my laundry out on the pole in the courtyard, I headed to the local public bath for the first time in ages. On the way, an unpleasant incident occurred which seemed to have been lying in wait expressly for me. Carrying my washbowl, I was about to cross the Sanjō-dōri avenue when a middle-aged guy on a motorbike waiting at the light spotted me.

"Oh, you, *sentō* okay? Ha, ha, ha!" he laughed his head off in a silly parody of English.

Losing my temper, I shouted back at him in Kansai dialect, "Yeah, that's right! Sorry, but even foreigners gotta wash from time to time.

That *sentō*'s really big, and no matter how long ya soak in the tubs it's the same price. Afterwards, ya can treat yourself to the massage chair for ten minutes for a measly twenty yen. It's awesome. Ya might try taking a bath yourself once in a while."

Completely flabbergasted, the guy sped off without even noticing that the light hadn't yet changed to green.

Gosh, what rubbish! Man has set foot on the moon, and the Berlin Wall has fallen. How many generations will it take before people in this town manage to change their mentality even one iota?

New Year's Eve was a quiet night.

I turned on the kerosene heater, sat down at the *kotatsu*, and set to work on my report. The room, lit up as it was by the faint glow of the heater, had an ethereal quality to it. The topic of the report was unusually interesting: from details in the story, we had to surmise the age of the "Sensei" character in Natsume Sōseki's *Kokoro* (The Heart of Things).

So during this tranquil final night of the year, I turned into a 2.7-millimeter-tall detective, burrowed into a reprint edition of *Kokoro* purchased long ago in Jinbō-chō, and wandered through various places of late Meiji Japan in search of literary clues to the puzzle. Every now and then, I returned to reality, switched on the TV, and flipped through the channels. Every station was broadcasting the same puerile garbage. Switching off the TV with a sigh, I couldn't suppress my exasperation at the fact that we'd be shown this sort of junk for the entire holiday season.

The Chion-in temple bells began ringing out the old year. The somber timbres sounded peculiarly lonesome. They nonetheless struck a positive tone in my heart, for I sensed something peaceful and warm in them. I could hear the laughter and footsteps of people along the Shirakawa river heading off for *hatsumōde*, the first prayer of the year at a temple or a shrine. The kerosene smell of my heater permeated the room, so I opened the window and let in some fresh cold air.

By checking the personal history of each character against the historical setting of the novel, I had no trouble solving the riddle. After taking my time writing out a clean copy, I was finished with the task a little after seven in the morning.

When I opened the window again, the new year was already in motion. Its peculiar scent flowed into my room like an early morning ocean breeze stealing into a harbor.

I went downstairs and took a long piss as I breathed in the fresh air of New Year's Day. As I pulled up my zipper, I realized how eager I was to see Kyōko. I wasn't at all tired, and my head was surprisingly clear. Nevertheless, when I returned to my room and lay down, I ended up sleeping for nearly five hours.

I returned to the kitchen and washed my face in the sink with cold water. I noticed a stack of *nengajō* New Year's greeting postcards on the refrigerator. They had been carefully divided into bundles, each bound with a rubber band. The thinnest bundle was mine.

I tossed on my leather jacket over a heavy sweater and walked to Mister Donut. The shop was thronging with customers returning from their *hatsumōde*. There were old people, rich people, children dressed in kimonos, and many other folks I usually never saw in the place. Running this type of business on New Year's Day must be as easy and rewarding as snatching ten-thousand-yen notes raining down from the sky.

I ordered four donuts, coffee, and orange juice, and sat down at a vacant counter seat. I started by wolfing down a couple of donuts, and then downed half the orange juice. When that was done, I pulled the bundle of *nengajō* out of my pocket. I took a sip of coffee, and as I ate the remaining two donuts, I read the postcards one by one.

The last one was from Kyōko.

> HAPPY NEW YEAR!
> I know it's not the Year of the Rabbit, but I'm sure this will be a wonderful year for you and Steevie. Please be sure to visit often again this year. Two beautiful women are anxiously waiting for you. Ha, ha, ha!

Kyōko's mother had obviously written the card, but the message was undeniably Kyōko's. I smiled, shoved the postcards back in my jacket pocket, gulped down the last bit of cold coffee, and left.

"Happy New Year, Kyōko."

Kyōko looked thinner than several weeks ago, and her straight black hair was longer. She wore jeans and a sweater with a Norwegian design. Although it suited her, the sweater looked like something you'd expect

Santa's secretary to be wearing. It suggested more a northern European Christmas than the Japanese New Year. Little reindeer were dashing from right to left across the gentle protuberance in the middle of her chest.

She said nothing in reply.

I glimpsed inside the plastic box in the corner of the living room. Steevie, curled up towards the back, was staring out at us with a calm and satisfied expression.

Kyōko pulled her hands out from under the *kotatsu* and reached out for my face. With the accuracy of a precision instrument, her slender fingers probed my forehead, cheeks, and lips. It was a gentle and innocent touch. Finally, she touched my bottom lip with her index finger as if to check that it was protruding properly. The next moment, she tenderly stole a kiss from the lips she had silently outlined. "Happy New Year," she said with a smile.

It was past three o'clock when we started eating. As promised, I talked about my experiences working on the yakuza project. Kyōko listened while concentrating on picking out some favorite items from the vast array of New Year delicacies with her chopsticks. She was as mysterious and beautiful as ever.

Saké was served halfway through the meal, and we shared a toast. After swallowing the first two or three proffered cups, I became so talkative I even surprised myself. As Kyōko and her mother listened to the story of Kaizuka-*oyabun*'s childhood, they became serious and bit their lips. But when I told about the gorilla punching himself in the face with his watermelon-sized fists, they both burst out laughing.

In the middle of my story, Kyōko quietly began searching for my hand. I didn't realize what she was doing at first. After landing on my shoulder, the palm of her hand slid down my arm—as if conducting a body search at an airport. For a split second, I exchanged glances with Kyōko's mother across the *kotatsu*. She smiled in a somewhat bashful way. It was the first time I ever saw such a look on her face. My heart throbbed for no reason. Almost immediately, however, a twinkle appeared in the corner of her eye, and she regained her composure.

Kyōko was checking my fingers.

"That's good," she said, laughing. "You still have all of them."

Kyōko's mother and I laughed, too.

"Oh, they'd never force someone from the outside world to chop off a finger," I said. After a moment of reflection, I added, "At least I don't think so."

"Is that right? How boring!" And with a bored look, she released my hand.

We drank late into the night, and all three of us got extremely drunk. I glanced at my watch, but I was so plastered, it took a while to get the hour hand into focus. It was definitely past one.

"I guess I should get going," I said, feeling that I had worn out my welcome.

"It's rather late," said Kyōko's mother, laying her hand on my arm. "Why don't you spend the night here? If you catch a cold or get sick now, you won't be able to finish that important thesis of yours."

"Oh, I really don't want to—" I started to protest, but Kyōko cut me off.

"It's no imposition at all. We have futons, and we'll just include your room fee in the bill for your dinner." Then she added in her usual mischievous way, "Or are you scared of sleeping under the same roof with two women?"

It was decided that I'd sleep in the small living room, so we pushed the *kotatsu* into a corner and laid out a futon next to Steevie's box. Left alone in my futon, I surveyed the room, which was wrapped in dreamy moonlight. Apart from the muted sound of Steevie munching his food, an unreal silence hung over the house.

Released from the tension and excitement of the past several weeks, and from that eerie, frightful desire never to return to Kyōto that I had felt in the tattooing room, I drifted into a state of pleasant intoxication. In the dim room, I recalled the New Year's postcard from Kyōko, smiled, and sank into a deep slumber bordering on unconsciousness.

I had no idea how much time had elapsed. Sensing a presence in the room, I awoke from my dreamless sleep. Barely conscious, I rolled over and discovered that Kyōko was there.

She had snuck into my futon and snuggled up next to me. She was completely naked.

For a second, I thought I was dreaming. But the heavy mass of silky hair against my face, the warmth emanating from her body, and that scent of vanilla mixed with incense were undeniably real. I reached my arms around her back and gently pulled her close.

"Were you awake?" she whispered in my ear.

"What's wrong?"

"I was a little lonely, but then something occurred to me: if we spend the first night of the year together, we're bound to spend many more together during the rest of the year, aren't we?"

She reached out, felt for my face with her fingertips, and kissed me softly on the lips.

"Wouldn't it be lovely to wake up tomorrow thinking that some mysterious fairy of the night had crept into your dreams?"

"Sure, it'd be lovely. But with a fairy so close and so naked, I doubt I'll be able to sleep."

I gulped.

She ignored my comment and slowly slid down towards the bottom of the futon. Without warning, she reached between my legs and began caressing me. Resisting the surge of happiness and excitement overcoming me, I tried to pull her back into my arms. But she softly resisted.

"My mother will hear us, so don't move."

She slid along my stomach to below my waist. I closed my eyes and forgot about the moon, now lighting the room from a sharper angle than before, as well as the living room enveloped in silence. Captivated and confused by the sensation of Kyōko's fingers and lips, I let myself be carried by an irresistible current. Before long, she had me in her mouth and began to lead me to orgasm. The torrent intensified into unnavigable wild oceans. Shaking with pleasure, I rode the waves until I experienced a *petite mort*—and the storm grew calm.

The short New Year holiday over, I put my nose to the grindstone and set to work on my graduation thesis, which had been hanging over my head like a black cloud. The more frantically I plunged into my studies, the more the thesis and its deadline began to develop into an obsession that dominated every aspect of my life.

At first, I continued visiting Kyōko and reading her novels by Kaikō Takeshi, Murakami Haruki, and other authors completely unrelated to my research. But as my thesis began to weigh more heavily on my mind, I lost the ability to concentrate and eventually gave up my visits altogether.

At that time, we had a lot of snow. It was moist and wet, the kind that doesn't stick to the ground. Gray, lonely-looking clouds hung low in the sky, and that distinctive Kyōto chill infiltrated every corner of the house. My kerosene heater burned steadily but didn't warm my room in the least, so I always felt cold.

It was late at night in the middle of February.

The guys playing mahjong in the *kura* storage house next door were busy making their usual racket. The top of my desk, scattered with dictionaries, reference books, sheets of paper and writing materials, looked like a battleground model laid out in an army's headquarters.

Fed up with the rowdy bozos next door, I searched for my earplugs amidst the clutter on my desk. I finally found a pair inside my Japanese thesaurus. They had been sandwiched there so long that they seemed to be permanently squashed into bizarre shapes. They were so dirty you'd never guess they had originally been yellow. Disregarding these minor details, I rolled them into little balls and shoved them deep into my ears. A few millimeters more and they'd have scraped against my brain. The room was immediately swallowed up in muffled silence.

For me, writing this thesis was the most tedious and uninteresting task in the world. Even so, I never questioned the meaning or necessity of what I was doing. I spent every day and night plowing through convoluted academic papers and weaving intriguing quotes into my text. With less than two weeks until the deadline, I spent every hour in irritation and anxiety. I cut all my lectures, took time off from my part-time job, and shut myself up in my disheveled room, with the futon left spread out on the floor night and day. My room became frighteningly dirty, and amidst this filth, enduring a perplexing pain in the pit of my stomach and chronic stiffness in my shoulders, I struggled to finish the fifty-page thesis.

As I stared at the *tokonoma* decorative alcove before my eyes, I began to have doubts. Sequestered in my room every day, never taking a walk, and rarely even doing any shopping, I was living with my head buried in this project. Now that I thought of it, I hadn't seen Kyōko for two weeks. What the hell was I doing? What possible purpose could this serve?

A two-word answer sprung to mind: "intellectual masturbation."

I first heard the expression from an old friend when he graduated from university several years ago.

It was during a peaceful afternoon in early summer. My friend had just submitted a difficult master's thesis entitled, "Conceptions of Death in the Work of Goethe," a task that had been running him ragged for over two years. We were lying on the campus grass in front of a large wall with a row of statues depicting important figures of the Protestant Reformation. I was staring at a squirrel dashing back and forth through the branches of a tall maple tree.

My friend had managed to get his thesis submitted, but at the cost of becoming mentally and physically exhausted. His face was pale, his cheeks were sunken, and his empty eyes were encircled with ghastly rings.

"Well, that's two years of intellectual masturbation behind me," he said with a sigh.

I stared at him in silence. I was amused, but I couldn't really fathom what he meant.

"You know what, over the past two years I've just been playing with myself," he continued. "By fooling around with queer arguments and theories, and forcing my own quirky interpretations on Goethe—who never could have even imagined my existence—I've been able to twist his work to suit my perverted aims and plunge into my own little fantasy world. That's all I've been doing for the past two years. Calling it literary research makes it sound important, but in the end, it's essentially masturbation."

The squirrel, circling around the trunk of the maple tree, worked his way towards dizzying heights. As I watched his nimble maneuverings, I waited for my friend to continue.

"My conclusions probably go way beyond the actual meaning of Goethe's texts. They're completely removed from his intentions and nothing more than the result of my own arbitrary ideas. The whole endeavor was utterly lacking in creativity and depressingly meaningless. That's how I feel about it now."

I lost sight of the squirrel and glanced over at my friend. He looked depressed but forced himself to smile.

"It's like letting your imagination run wild about some cute girl who's a complete stranger, just so you can jerk off. So how is that any different from masturbation?"

I could see his point.

"Right, intellectual masturbation…" I repeated the expression with some admiration.

Sitting in my small room in Kyōto, ten thousand kilometers from that plot of grass, I recalled our conversation. Quoting from academic articles I barely understood, and trying to come up with some newfangled interpretation, I wondered if I wasn't merely repeating that sterile and depraved procedure my friend had referred to as *intellectual masturbation*.

I got more and more depressed.

It was pitch-black outside. Thanks to the earplugs, the world was absolutely silent, apart from the strange sound inside my own head which was similar to the low hum of a submarine engine. The square window of the *kura* across the alleyway was lit up. They were still playing mahjong. I told myself I must be the only person in the world working on a thesis on such a cold February night.

I turned back to the gridded Japanese manuscript paper on my desk. The stream of small characters running vertically down the page stopped at the bottom of the second line—like lava that had suddenly hardened due to a rise in the land. The left part of the page was hopelessly blank and spacious. It resembled the white expanse you see flying over Siberia in the dead of winter.

I picked up my pencil again and for the next several hours concentrated on my work. Just as I was starting to forget about the outside world, a loud noise found its way through my earplugs. I figured that Steevie, sensing the first signs of hunger, was sending an SOS to his owner, who had forgotten both his existence and the replenishment that supported that existence. I decided to ignore his distress signal until I reached an appropriate place to stop.

There was another big thump. That broke the camel's back! Imagining how I would cook up the plump little fellow, I slammed my pencil down and moved to get up.

When I lifted my head, I nearly had a heart attack. Someone was standing in the dimly lit entrance of the room.

It was Kyōko.

But it took a while for this fact to sink in. I couldn't speak. Other than the violent beating of my heart, everything seemed to have come to a standstill.

Gradually, my brain kicked into motion. What I had assumed to be the noise of Steevie's brazen revolt were actually the sounds of Kyōko opening and closing the rackety ground floor door, feeling her way along the hallway, and climbing up the steep wooden staircase. The loud thump that had jolted me back to reality from the needless fretting over my paper must have been her shutting the door after entering the room.

"Hey, you scared me no end!" I shrieked at Kyōko, who was standing in front of the door. "Almost had a heart attack!"

She said something in reply, but no sound came from her moving lips.

I remembered that I was wearing earplugs and yanked them out. I stood up and gently pulled Kyōko into my arms.

"You really surprised me," I told her.

"I *meant* to surprise you," she said with a straight face.

I laughed. "Well, you certainly succeeded."

What surprised me the most, though, was that she'd been able to walk all this way so late at night. Of course, she'd been to my house many times before, but I couldn't get over the fact that she'd managed to walk all this way by herself—along pitch-black streets on a moonless night.

Just when I was about to ask about this, I shut my mouth and hugged her more tightly. What an imbecile! What was wrong with me? For Kyōko, it certainly didn't make much difference whether it was a moonless winter night or a mid-summer afternoon.

There was a short silence.

"Sorry I startled you like this. But I called many times, and I couldn't get through. I was worried, so I dropped by to check on you." Her warm breath brushed past my neck as she spoke.

"I haven't paid my phone bill for a while. It's probably been disconnected."

Kyōko slightly pulled back from me.

"It's cold. I'm frozen to the bones. Hey, why don't we go to the public bath?"

I glanced at my watch. It was eleven thirty. If we hurried, we could make it in time. I rubbed my neck with my hand. The area below my chin felt so grungy it reminded me of the unshaven face of PLO Chairman Yasser Arafat.

"Let's do it. I can certainly use a wash."

I placed soap, shampoo, a razor, a toothbrush, and toothpaste into my washbowl, and laid two folded towels on top. Then I placed Kyōko's hand on my elbow, and we headed out.

The evening air was chilly. We hurried along the short distance to the bathhouse. When we arrived, I handed Kyōko a towel, told her we should give each other a yell when we're finished, and held open the door to the women's section for her.

I entered the men's side. The few bathers that remained were getting ready to head home. "Good evenin', and welcome!" said the woman on the watcher's seat in her usual friendly tone. As I handed her the money for the two of us, I said, "I'd appreciate it if you'd keep an eye on my friend."

I was alone before I knew it. When I turned around after showering off, everyone was gone. The clock on the wall said twelve o'clock. I peeked into the changing room and noticed that the woman had taken down the *noren* short split curtain at the entrance, and was cleaning outside.

At that moment, I became distinctly conscious of a kinky impulse welling up in me: I wanted to see Kyōko naked without her noticing. From the other side of the partition wall, I could hear the sound of splashing water and the light breathing of someone enjoying a bath. These sounds gave me an overly vivid image of Kyōko's body.

Stepping on the narrow tile edge for soap and other toiletries, just above the row of faucets, I pulled myself up against the wall. By standing on my tiptoes, I could see the other side. I was able to execute the maneuver with surprising speed and agility, without any superfluous movements.

As expected, Kyōko was the only one there. She stood drying herself with a towel. Her long, wet hair was draped over her shoulder, hiding her right breast. Tracing the gentle curves of her body, she slowly wiped away the innumerable droplets that glittered radiantly on her skin.

Kyōko's body was beautiful beyond imagination. She felt for the rim of the bath, lifted a leg to place her foot on it, and patted down her firm thigh with the towel. In a state of dazed excitement, I stared at her profile, shoulders, chest, and legs. Some soapsuds remained on the calf of her raised leg. Her flesh was smooth and womanly. Completely calm, she smiled, lowered her leg, and dried her crotch.

I became uncontrollably excited, and a certain part of my anatomy bumped against the wall. No matter how friendly the woman at the entrance might be, if she were to catch me like this, it'd be more than a bit awkward. I scurried down from the wall and took a cold shower.

When we got back to the boarding house, I used my lips to trace every nook and cranny of the body Kyōko had so scrupulously dried. The touch and scent drove me wild, and my heart leapt for joy. Kyōko smiled, wrapped her arms around me, and pulled me down lower. I could feel her fingertips digging into my flesh. Softly holding her down by the hips, I slid down the smooth, tender terrain of her stomach. I could hear her panting above me.

"You know, I was watching you in the bath," I confessed facing the gentle slope below me. She pulled my face close to hers, smiled, and with her usual precision, kissed me on the lips.

"I was aware of that."

"Really? You knew all along?"

"So my body, how was it?"

I pulled back, and by the dim light of the kerosene heater, took another look at her.

"You've got a very nice body."

"Even compared to other women?"

"There are some individual differences," I started off, somewhat at a loss. "But most bodies are about the same."

"So my body's nothing special?"

"Oh no, it's definitely very special," I said, embracing her as tightly as I could.

The heater had gone out without my noticing. Nevertheless, a definite warmth still hung in the air. I pulled Kyōko's sweater over my naked body, stood up, and opened the window slightly. Next door, the storage house was quiet. Further on, towards the Sanjō-dōri avenue, I could see snow gently falling near the streetlights.

As I stared absentmindedly at my white breath being sucked out into the night, I realized that exactly a year had passed since I had first met Kyōko.

"We're really disappointed in you."

"That's right. We're really disappointed."

These were the first words spoken to me at my oral defense. Thrown out like a double punch, they hung in mid-air with a strange unreality.

The seminar room had a completely different atmosphere from usual. The desks were lined up in front of the windows, and my professor and a young assistant, both with disgruntled looks, were sitting behind one of them. In front of the row, stood a tiny, solitary stool. The whole arrangement created an unbelievably dreary mood.

Sitting on the stool gave me a taste of how an unjustly accused defendant must feel under the condemning stares of a jury. I tried to remember Koike's sexy legs, but the oppressive atmosphere easily squelched this feeble attempt to relax. The thesis I had struggled to write was lying on the table in front of me.

"We really are disappointed in you," repeated my professor, as if to rub it in further.

"To begin with, there is no way one could possibly overlook this error," said the young assistant, snatching up my thesis and pointing at the title with his shaky, slender finger. I squinted to see what the decisive mistake might be, but was too far away to discern the flaw he was indicating. Holding my thesis, he stood up and headed towards me, all the while avoiding looking me in the eye.

"This *kanji* is improperly written," he said in a bizarrely shrill tone of voice. "It's very slight, but you can distinctly make out that this top stroke is protruding on the right, which is undeniably incorrect." As he spoke, he kept staring behind me, which created the illusion that a jury might really be there. I inadvertently turned around, but of course no one was there.

"For a student majoring in Japanese literature to make a mistake in the Japanese of the title is nothing short of inexcusable."

Hell! What could I answer to that?

Next, my professor opened the thesis and spent an unbearable amount of time looking it over. I was so nervous that I wanted to shift my position, but even the slightest movement caused the stool to squeak and echo eerily in the classroom.

"You mention that the protagonist lived in Onomichi for a while," said my professor, finally lifting his eyes from the pages. "But if you don't mention the connection between this scene and the author's life, you completely miss the point of the novel."

"I covered that in detail in my footnotes . . ." I started to say, but then stopped. Footnotes? They obviously hadn't bothered to read them. No doubt about it. They certainly didn't go to so much trouble. And then it dawned on me. They probably hadn't even read the whole thesis. That's the gut feeling I got. They spent some time asking me questions, but rather than having my own knowledge tested, it became increasingly obvious that neither of them had properly read the thing. What a charade! Thoroughly disgusted, I gave tolerable answers to their questions and rushed from the classroom when the ordeal ended ten minutes later.

For a while, I just stood in the hallway dumbfounded. The unbearable stress that had built up while working on my thesis suddenly disappeared, and I felt like laughing out loud. Was this the conclusion to four years of study? Did I read all those books, write all those papers, and go through all that anxiety just for this kangaroo court of an oral exam? What a sinister joke! I was overcome by a sense of emptiness and meaninglessness, then gradually, began to get angry.

I traipsed down the hallway. Another student must have entered the classroom, but I had no idea who it was. I once again heard the scolding voice of my professor and the shrill voice of the assistant. I quickened my pace. Just then, an image of Kaizuka-*oyabun* came to mind. "Literature ain't somethin' you should be studyin' at college, is it?" he had said. You could say that again! I wanted to get out of there as quickly as possible.

The afternoon campus was thronging with students as usual. I saw some of my classmates dressed up for job interviews, but I wasn't in the mood for talking. Who gave a shit about literature, master's theses, and oral exams? Securing a job is the difficult part, graduating is just a formality. That's what their bright expressions were saying. Without even stopping off at *Dejima*, the lounge for foreign students, I headed straight to my scooter. The air was dreadfully cold, and the sky covering the city overcast.

When I arrived at Kyōko's house, she wasn't there. "She stepped out to do some shopping," said her mother. "But she'll be right back, so why don't you come in and wait?"

We had tea in the living room. Kyōko's mother made small talk. I responded the best I could, but I had other things on my mind. Noticing that I was distracted, she stopped talking. She gazed into my eyes, with that fond look she had always shown me, searching for an answer. But once she realized I wasn't about to open up, she went back to chatting in her cheerful voice.

Kyōko returned about thirty minutes later. With two large shopping bags in her hands, she looked radiant and cheerful, in complete contrast to me. Unable to sort out my feelings, I felt like someone trying to maneuver a boat with a broken rudder across a dark ocean. I was longing for something. For what I had no idea, but I had this intense craving for something.

Kyōko sat down at the *kotatsu* with us, and immediately asked, "So did your oral exam go well?" in a cheerful voice.

I didn't answer, but what I needed was slowly dawning on me. I kept silent and waited for my emotions to subside.

I finished my tea, and finally said, "Kyōko, let's read something."

Kyōko couldn't hide her surprise. "Now?" she replied, with an astounded look. "You want to read something now, at this precise moment?"

"Yes, I want to read right now, like we used to." I smiled.

It was only three or four o'clock in the afternoon, but the gloomy, lonely veil of twilight hung over the garden, and the neighboring house, with its low connecting passageway was beginning to fade from view.

"Well, then, have a pleasant reading," said Kyōko's mother, leaving the room.

I stood up, went to the bookcase full of old books, and searched for something appropriate. As I was holding books and reading opening passages, that feeling of discontent, a mixture of despondency and loss, which had been in me since the oral exam, gradually faded away. It was like watching the morning mist covering the plains of Mongolia slowly vanish into thin air.

I chose Abe Kōbō's *Suna no Onna* (The Woman in the Dunes) and returned to the *kotatsu*. To tell the truth, it could've been *The Little Prince*, *Gulliver's Travels*, or just about anything. I just wanted to immerse myself in the quiet literary mood I had shared with Kyōko so often in the past.

I crossed my legs and opened Abe's novel. The end of the bookmark ribbon was so dirty it looked like the tail of a mouse that had spent years wandering around a big city. After staring at the mouse-tail for a moment, I started reading.

I read fluently right from the beginning. It was such an auspicious start that I surprised even myself. The writing was easy to read, and my voice effortlessly carried the sounds to Kyōko's delicately shaped ears. I gradually regained my composure. The feeling of relief that washed over me had a momentum similar to that of the tide being drawn in by the moon's gravity. I had no difficulty reading aloud, but I hardly paid any attention to the content. It wasn't that I couldn't grasp the meaning; it was just that comprehension wasn't all that important. I was trying to recreate a certain type of atmosphere, and the book's content was only secondary.

I found myself thinking about unrelated matters. I slipped into reflections about my four years as a foreign student. And not being the clever type that can read while thinking about something else, my recitation screeched to an abrupt halt.

"Finished already?" asked Kyōko with the same stunned expression as before.

I didn't answer. Reading Abe's novel, I became aware of all sorts of things—that had absolutely nothing to do with its content. It was difficult to put into words, but at that moment, something struck me as if I had run into a wall… Kyōto was a lifeless city.

Both the imaginary world that I had created for myself and the actual city that existed in the literal sense were irrevocably dead. I had expected much and anticipated so many discoveries here. But in the end, I had gained nothing. It was a dead kingdom.

With the city scenery and people's stares in the background, all kind of images flashed through my mind: the Berlin Wall, the tattooing room, the title of my master's thesis, and more. And then I knew: in the near future, I'd have to escape this stagnant place and return to my nomadic lifestyle.

"Hello! Anybody home? What's wrong?" Kyōko's voice reached me as if from a distance.

"Sorry, I was thinking about something." I picked up the book again. If at that precise moment, I had simply told her what was on my mind, we probably would have separated in a completely different manner. But for better or worse, I let the opportunity go by. At that moment, I wasn't thinking that far ahead.

After that, I spent nearly two hours reading *The Woman in the Dunes*. Emptying my head, not holding back or adding anything, I simply read the sentences aloud: "There was no need to hurry to escape. The round-trip ticket he now held in his hand was blank, and he could fill in the destination and point of return however he wished."

I had never read aloud for so long. Surprisingly, however, I never tired. Apart from my voice, the small living room was completely silent. Everything was still, except for Kyōko's quiet blinking and the movement of my hand turning the pages. At some point, I was struck by the illusion that my voice was not my voice, and that Abe Kōbō's novel had lost its reality as a novel.

That was our last session of face-to-face reading.

I decided to put in an appearance at my graduation ceremony. It seemed like a necessary ritual to bring my life as a student to a symbolic close. I had been looking forward to this day for four years, but the event failed to move me. I felt as miserable and frustrated as if I were attending the wedding of an old girlfriend who had ended up with another guy.

My friend in the English literature department, apparently having graduated with top honors, appeared on stage as the class representative. Bowing nervously to the university president, he accepted his diploma. After that, we listened to the president's long-winded speech.

"In the long life that lies ahead of you, you will run into many difficulties. You will have to suffer hardships, and you will have to crawl through the mud. But without complaint, you must do your best, never abandoning the pursuit of truth and of noble purposes. It is only by overcoming adversity that one can truly appreciate the beauty of a blue sky..."

Jeez! When you're sending off hundreds of students facing bleak futures, you might want to be a little more positive about it, even if it requires a lie or two. But to tell the truth, Kyōko's call the previous evening was weighing on my mind much more than the president's speech.

"I decided to take the job after all," she had said. "Today, I got a phone call from the personnel department of that company which had offered me a position. They wanted an answer. They hadn't heard from me for a long time, so they were beginning to wonder. It seems they've never hired any blind staff before, so there's a lot of things they need to prepare."

I had not said anything.

"Of course, I told them I accept. For a long time, I just didn't know what to do. My current life of just lounging around is easy and lots of fun, but I'm not going anywhere. I don't have any goals or sense of direction. That sometimes makes me feel very insecure."

I had painfully understood what she meant, but for a moment I had not responded.

"I think it's wonderful that you're trying new things. Knowing you, I'm sure you'll do a great job."

"You really think so? So even if I take the job, you'll continue offering me your unconditional support? You know, Tōkyō's not that far away. We could meet whenever you like." She appeared to be already dreaming about living there.

"Well, I guess so," I had answered vaguely, somehow feeling that Kyōko's decision had also sealed my fate.

When the president's speech, which was more in the tone of a memorial service, finally petered to an end, all the Japanese literature students headed to a classroom in the adjacent building. We turned in our student IDs and received our diplomas in exchange. It was an extremely businesslike transaction, completely devoid of emotion. Good grief! It was as if we were just swapping pieces of paper. A far cry from the flamboyance and joy of an American ceremony, where a thousand graduation caps are tossed in unison high into the blue sky and then come tumbling down again onto a beautiful green lawn.

With my purple hard-covered diploma under my arm, I headed out into the hallway and gazed at the scenery from the window. It was a beautiful morning, but a strong wind was blowing. The tops of the trees in the Kyōto Imperial Palace were swaying like innumerable green waves. I spotted a young couple walking hand-in-hand on the gravel path below the trees, and my heart ached.

I wanted to embark on a new journey in search of sceneries that would quell the yearning in my heart. I knew the time had come for me to talk about this to Kyōko.

I saw Kyōko for the last time on the evening before she left for Tōkyō. There was a large full moon shining overhead as we sat on a bench in Maruyama Park. As she perhaps suspected what I was going to say, she had left a very small, yet unusual space between us.

In as precise terms as possible, I explained why I had been wanting to leave Japan.

"I'm tired of this city. I'm sure it's a great place for sightseeing, but I just can't blend in."

Probably because I was overly conscious of hurting Kyōko, the necessary words slipped out of my reach and stubbornly refused to come back.

"How should I put it? Ever since I came here, I've been searching for something extremely Japanese, longing for acceptance in a new, unknown world. But contrary to my expectations, this town just hasn't accepted me. At least, that's how I feel. I don't know why I get so worked up about it. It's really strange. There must be something about this country—or about this city—that makes foreigners feel this way. Maybe I'm just too different from my surroundings, or maybe I've been trying too hard to create a special niche for myself where everyone would accept me."

Kyōko stirred the gravel beneath the bench with the toe of her shoe.

"That's a bit unfair, don't you think?" she argued. "I mean, Kyōto certainly does have a peculiar atmosphere. But a town, where all kinds of different people live, is not something that has a will of its own, is it?"

"Of course, you're right. When it gets right down to it, my feeling that I haven't been accepted is just my own subjective, personal bias. But whether it's a persecution complex, or whatever…"

I held my breath for a second.

"… I want to leave."

Kyōko's feet stopped moving. I sensed the tension in her body. An expression of loneliness and pain crossed her face. This emotion broke through as naturally as when she used to yield to waves of pleasure.

"Leave… where will you go?" she asked in a dry tone of voice.

I again searched for the right words. "I don't know yet, but I need to move on. As long as I stay here, I'll feel different and out of place. If I don't make a change, things will get bad. I can just feel it. If I stay any longer, I'm going to be crushed." Once the words were spoken, they seemed to linger in the air surrounding us.

"Well, then, let's go to Tōkyō together. You've graduated, so I'm sure you could get a job. Even I managed to find something."

I was silent.

Kyōko read my mind with the same penetrating insight as the fortunetellers in the park.

"No, that's not it, is it?" she said, in a sad and faintly trembling voice. "You want to spread your wings and go somewhere far away on your own, don't you?"

Though I knew explanations wouldn't alleviate her sadness, rationalizing came out before I knew it.

"Last autumn, when I saw the fall of the Berlin Wall on TV, something changed in me that can never be reversed."

Kyōko didn't say anything.

"On that evening, I realized I was facing two walls. One was the wall that the people were knocking down. And when it fell, I could hear the world calling me from the other side. That's right, the actual Berlin Wall. When I saw it on TV, I knew: I wanted to return to my former lifestyle. I had to get moving.

"The other wall was more abstract. It was this haunting wall that I kept running into in my everyday life here in Kyōto. It also occurred to me that Kyōto is a city of walls. Earthen walls. Bamboo fences. Bamboo blinds. Lattices. All these things that I'd once considered beautiful began to look like symbols of the walls in the hearts of the people here."

Kyōko sighed.

"I can understand what you mean. I've often felt something similar myself."

"Anyway, it's really been wearing me out. Living here, I feel like I'm constantly yearning for something—"

"Hold on," Kyōko interrupted. Her voice rang out firm and clear in the hushed park. "Did you also feel that way when you were with me?"

"No, with you it's different. I always feel at peace when I'm with you. I still do right now. But I need to go. I'd like to find a place where it's *normal to be different*, where *being different is the rule of the game*. Living here has become—what else can I say?—just suffocating."

Kyōko turned to face me.

“I’m sorry. I should have noticed earlier that you were agonizing over this sort of thing.”

“Don’t be. There’s no way you could have known. I have just become aware of it myself. Don’t worry about it.”

Her eyes, shining in the cool light of the full moon, were pleading. They were trying to say something. Had I forgotten that these eyes couldn’t see? No, it wasn’t that I had forgotten. At that precise moment, Kyōko was in fact *looking* at me. I knew it for a fact.

Kyōko was crying. I unconsciously reached out to wipe her tears away, but she gently—though with determination—pushed my hand back.

“I’m sorry, I didn’t mean to cry. I don’t want to hold you back. But I’m not strong enough just to say goodbye and wish you well. I wanted more time.”

I searched my mind for something more to say, but there was nothing. Kyōko wiped her tears with her own hand, then gave me a little smile.

“I wanted to go to the karaoke bar again. I wanted to try that *miso champon* of yours. I also wanted to try smoking a pipe.”

I didn’t reply.

“Say,” said Kyōko, placing her hand on my arm. “Will you write me a letter from time to time, from wherever in the world you happen to be?”

For a second, I felt something warm welling up in my chest.

“But I’ll have to have one of my co-workers read it for me, so don’t write anything *too* suggestive.” As she said this, she flashed me that mischievous grin of hers.

She squeezed my hand, and I squeezed her hand back. Holding hands in silence, we sat perfectly still for a long time. It was as if we were recharging our batteries to face the lives lying ahead of us.

After a while, she stood up.

And for the first time, I saw her take her white cane from her bag. When she took it in her hand, it snapped out in a zig-zag pattern. It really did resemble a *nunchaku*.

Tapping the ground in front of her with the cane, Kyōko headed towards the park’s entrance. Watching her, I strongly felt that beyond those gates, a bright and tangible future was awaiting her.

I looked up at the full moon. The tears in my eyes made it difficult to imagine my own future. Still sitting on the bench, I stared and stared through the darkness at the silent moon, which refused to give me even a clue. Then it dimly occurred to me: on the other side of the planet, it was already daytime.

Translator's comments

Written in Japanese by a non-native speaker of the language, *Ichigensan* tells the story of an unnamed foreign student studying at a university in Kyōto and his relationship with a blind Japanese woman named Kyōko. First published in Tōkyō in 1997, it was hailed for its sensual descriptions, brilliant metaphors, and witty observations. The novel won the Subaru Prize for Literature and was nominated for the Akutagawa Prize, the most prestigious literary award in Japan. In 1999, the novel was made into a beautifully shot movie, starring Suzuki Honami, a popular Japanese actress, and Edward Atterton, a British actor who once lived in Japan.

The setting of *Ichigensan* reflects the experiences of its author, David Zoppetti, who studied at Dōshisha University in the late 1980s, a time that roughly corresponds to the period of Japan's "bubble economy," which collapsed in 1991. Not only is *Ichigensan* a poignant love story, it also focuses on the idiosyncrasies of the inhabitants of one specific city, Kyōto. For over a thousand years, up until the 1868 transfer of the imperial court to Tōkyō (formerly Edo), Kyōto was the capital of Japan. Kyōto's citizens have long been exceedingly proud of their cultural heritage. Although Kyōto is without a doubt Japan's most popular tourist destination, its residents are known to be somewhat discriminatory and rather closed not only to foreigners, but also to any Japanese not originally from the city.

The title of the novel reflects this peculiar Kyōto attitude. In Kyōto usage, the word "ichigensan" refers to first-time customers who attempt to enter an establishment without a proper introduction. Even today, the "ichigensan okotowari" (no first-time customers allowed) policy is still in effect for Kyōto's more exclusive geisha teahouses and restaurants, though the economic downturn has resulted in some relaxation of this policy. Although the expression "ichigensan" does not itself appear in the novel, it clearly refers to the unnamed narrator and protagonist "Boku" (the pronoun a male speaker uses to refer to himself). The novel exposes the narrator's frustrations when seeking admission to the innermost recesses of the city, its culture, and its people.

The situation Zoppetti depicts as distinctive to Kyōto, however, mirrors a phenomenon common to all of Japan. Since the early 1980s, *kokusaika* (internationalization) had been the watchword of Japan's educational reforms. The Plan to Accept 100,000 International Students was implemented in 1983, the Japan International Cooperation Agency

(JICA) began opening international training centers throughout Japan, and the Japan Exchange and Teaching (JET) program started in 1987. However, as *Ichigensan* makes clear, Japanese people continued to have difficulty accepting foreigners into society. As one who has lived in Japan since 1990, I can attest to the fact that Zoppetti's depiction of how Westerners tend to be treated is right on the mark. Indeed, what initially moved me about the novel was that I felt that someone had for the first time truly understood and expressed how it feels for Westerners to live here—especially for those who attempt to immerse themselves in the culture and to interact with Japanese in their own language. With the increasing impact of globalization, the situation has definitely improved, but with Japan now debating the need to change its immigration policies and accept more foreigners, the novel's underlying themes are as relevant today as when the novel was first published.

Ichigensan has sometimes been categorized as being *ekkyō bungaku* (border-crossing literature), a genre that includes other non-Japanese writers of Japanese literature, such as Hideo Levy, Arthur Binard, Kaneshiro Kazuki, and more recently, Yang Yi and Shirin Nezammafi. For better or worse, the Japanese media has made much of the fact that most of these authors are foreigners whose native language is not Japanese. In ways similar to the works of these other writers, *Ichigensan* questions the validity of the *kokusaika* paradigm, in which international exchange is always seen in terms of national identity, and the difference between insiders and outsiders is assumed to be obvious. In the case of Zoppetti's novel, the narrator and protagonist feels at home in Japanese culture, enjoys reading novels that ordinary Japanese readers would find challenging, and possesses an extraordinary command of the language. The novel's critique of the exclusive nature of Japanese society, therefore, is not made from the perspective of one with a strong opposing national identity, but from the perspective of one who strongly desires (mistakenly or not) to become part of that society. The protagonist is both an insider and an outsider at the same time.

Ichigensan poses numerous challenges for a translator. Given that the novel focuses on the protagonist's attempt to immerse himself in the Japanese culture he experiences in Kyōto, it is absolutely essential for the translation to convey to English readers a strong sense of that distinctly Japanese world. Therefore, Japanese terms, such as *tokonoma*, *hachimaki*, and *kotatsu*, which are intimately connected to Japanese culture and which have no appropriate English equivalents have been retained as often as possible. However, instead of relying on intrusive footnotes, I have tried to convey the meaning through context or with short glosses following the Japanese terms. To those familiar with Japanese culture, these glosses may appear to be superfluous, but I felt that such a compromise was necessary to make the novel accessible to all readers. For the same reason, I have followed the Modified Hepburn system of Romanization for Japanese words, with macrons used to indicate long vowels—even for place names, such as Tōkyō and Kyōto, which are often written without the macron. Additionally, for Japanese names, I followed the Japanese practice of listing the surname first.

Another difficulty I faced was in finding ways to capture in English the distinctive style of Japanese used by Zoppetti, especially his witty humor and turns of phrase. To tell the truth, these were the passages that underwent considerable revision. Fortunately, during the revision phase, I was in a translator's enviable position of being able to consult directly with the author, who also happens to be fluent in English. Zoppetti provided extensive criticism, comments, and suggestions for the entire translation—focusing especially on those passages that he himself felt were most characteristic of his style. As a result, I think we were able to come up with an aesthetically pleasing translation that captures the spirit and feel of the original novel.

Takuma Sminkey
Okinawa, February 2011

素民喜　琢磨
沖縄、2011 年 2 月

Other publications by Ōzaru Books

Sunflowers – Le Soleil

MURAI Shimako

A play in one act, translated from the Japanese by Ben Jones

Hiroshima is synonymous with the first hostile use of an atomic bomb. Many people think of this occurrence as one terrible event in the past, which is studied from history books. Shimako Murai and other 'Women of Hiroshima' believe otherwise: for them, the bomb had after-effects which affected countless people for decades, effects that were all the more menacing for their unpredictability – and often, invisibility.

This is a tale of two such people: on the surface successful modern women, yet each bearing underneath hidden scars as horrific as the keloids that disfigured Hibakusha on the days following the bomb.

ISBN: 978-0-9559219-3-3 Also on Kindle

The Body as a Vessel

The Methodology of Hijikata Tatsumi's Ankoku Butō

MIKAMI Kayo

An analysis of the modern dance form

Translated from the Japanese by Rosa van Hensbergen

When Hijikata Tatsumi's "Butō" appeared in 1959, it revolutionized not only Japanese dance but also the concept of performance art worldwide. It has however proved notoriously difficult to define or tie down. Mikami was a disciple of Hijikata for three years, and in this book, combines insights from these years with earlier notes from other dancers, to decode the ideas and processes behind butō.

ISBN: 978-0-9931587-4-2

Misadventures at Margate – A Legend of Jarvis's Jetty

Thomas Ingoldsby, illustrated by Ernest Jessop

This lavishly illustrated facsimile edition comprises a humorous story about the adventures of a 19th century London gentleman visiting the seaside resort of Margate. There he naively befriends a poor 'vulgar boy', only to have his trust betrayed...

Part of the ever-popular Ingoldsby Legends.

ISBN: 978-0-9931587-9-7

Other publications by Ōzaru Books

Turner's Margate Through Contemporary Eyes
The Viney Letters
Stephen Channing

Margate in the early 19th Century was an exciting town, where smugglers and 'preventive men' fought to outwit each other. One young man decided to set out for Australia to make his fortune in the Bendigo gold rush. Half a century later, he began writing for Keble's Gazette, describing Margate with great familiarity (and tremendous powers of recall). Viney's interests covered a huge range of topics, from Thanet folk customs, through diatribes on the perils of assigning intelligence to dogs, to geological theories including suggestions for the removal of sandbanks off the English coast "in obedience to the sovereign will and intelligence of man". This book also contains numerous contemporary illustrations.

ISBN: 978-0-9559219-2-6

The Margate Tales
Stephen Channing

Illuminating and entertaining accounts of Thanet in the 18th and early to mid 19th centuries, with content ranging from furious battles in the letters pages, to hilarious pastiches, witty poems and astonishing factual reports. Illustrated with over 70 drawings from the time, The Margate Tales brings the society of the time to life, and as with Chaucer's Canterbury Tales, demonstrates how in many areas, surprisingly little has changed.

ISBN: 978-0-9559219-5-7

Watch and Ward
Nigel Cruttenden

A comprehensive history of Margate Borough Police from its inception in 1858 until its amalgamation into Kent County Constabulary in 1943. It covers the origins of the modern police force, and is also an invaluable reference work for enthusiasts researching family history in and around Thanet. Full indices make it easy for modern Margatonians and Thanetians to check whether their ancestors might have been 'involved' with the police – on whichever side!

ISBN 978-1-915174-03-1

Other publications by Ōzaru Books

The Hooden Horse of East Kent – Annotated Edition

Percy Maylam

Percy Maylam's "The Hooden Horse: an East Kent Christmas Custom" was long the definitive work on Hoodening, and is indispensable even now, but the first format is very rare, and only a reduced edition appeared later. This new eBook includes the whole of Maylam's text, with numerous features to help those wanting to push the research further. This edition also contains updated versions of the early 20C photographs.

Available on Kindle

Discordant Comicals – The Hooden Horse of East Kent

George Frampton

Hoodening is an ancient calendar custom unique to East Kent, involving a wooden horse's head on a pole, carried by a man concealed by a sack. The earliest reliable record is from 1735, but other than Percy Maylam's seminal work "The Hooden Horse", little serious research has gone into the tradition. George Frampton has rectified this, by cross-referencing dozens of newspaper reports, census records and other accounts to build a comprehensive picture of who the Hoodeners were, why (and where) they did it, and how it related to other folk traditions. Full indices make it easy for modern Men and Maids of Kent to check whether their ancestors might have been involved, and detailed references make this an invaluable resource for social historians too. Over 70 full colour illustrations.

ISBN: 978-0-9559219-7-3

Animal Guising and the Kentish Hooden Horse

James Frost

This book builds on Maylam's "The Hooden Horse" and Frampton's "Discordant Comicals" to expand the field of study into East Kent's unique folk custom: what hoodening was, what the hooden horse is, and how it can be seen in the national context of animal guising. It covers historical records and artifacts, revival groups, "Autohoodening" performances which reimagine the old tradition in a modern context, and related practices such as the Mari Lwyd. Appendices contain the text of numerous contemporary verses and plays. Over 60 full colour illustrations, many never seen before in print.

ISBN: 978-1-915174-06-2

Other publications by Ōzaru Books

A Victorian Cyclist – Rambling through Kent in 1886

Stephen & Shirley Channing

For the late Victorians, "velocipedes" were a novelty disparaged as being unhealthy and unsafe – indeed tricycles were for a time seen as more likely to succeed. Some people however adopted the newfangled devices with alacrity, embarking on adventurous tours throughout the countryside.

One of them documented his 'rambles' around East Kent in such detail that it is still possible to follow his routes on modern cycles, and compare the fauna and flora (and pubs!) with those he vividly described. Over 200 illustrations, complemented by a fully updated website.

ISBN: 978-0-9559219-7-1 Also available on Kindle

Bicycle Beginnings
And what people of the 19C were really saying about it

Stephen Channing

The best way to get a feel for what early 'velocipedists' encountered is to read the words of the times, and this book gathers into one volume the most enlightening, entertaining and extraordinary insights from contemporary sources.

The mammoth work (over 190,000 words, covering the period 1779 to 1912) contains race reports, legal developments, technical innovations and inventions, records, advertisements, acrobatics, clothing, poems, arguments for and against the new-fangled vehicles, debates over women cyclists, and a long travelogue, "Berlin to Budapest on a Bicycle" capturing the excitement of a forgotten age of adventure on two wheels.

Not all the inventions were two-wheeled, however. This book also reveals the numerous variations that came into being before makers standardized on the shapes we commonly see nowadays: tricycles, ice velocipedes, water-paddle hobby-horses... These are explained with the aid of numerous illustrations, covering the gamut from cartoons to technical drawings and photographs. Even the race reports demonstrate far more variety than we are accustomed to seeing: 'ordinaries' (penny farthings) versus 'safety' bicycles versus tandems, monocycles, dwarf cycles, tricycles, double tricycles, four-wheel velocipedes, horses, ice skaters, steamships...

ISBN: 978-1-5210-8632-2 Also available on Kindle

Other publications by Ōzaru Books

Sally Aviss

The Cairnmor Trilogy

Book 1: The Call of Cairnmor
Book 2: Changing Tides, Changing Times
Book 3: Where Gloom and Brightness Meet

The Scottish Isle of Cairnmor is a place of great beauty and undisturbed wilderness, a haven for wildlife, a land of white sandy beaches and inland fertile plains. To this remote island comes a stranger, Alexander Stewart, on a quest to solve the disappearance of two people and their unborn child.

In the dense jungle of Malaya in 1942, Doctor Rachel Curtis stumbles across a mysterious, unidentifiable stranger, close to death. *Changing Times, Changing Tides* introduces new personalities, in a unique combination of novel and history that tells a story of love, loss, friendship and heroism as the characters are shaped by the ebb and flow of WW2.

The final book in the Cairnmor Trilogy takes the action forward into the late 1960s. It is a story of heartbreak and redemptive love, reflecting the conflicting attitudes, problems and joys of a liberating era.

ISBN: 978-0-9559219-9-5 / 978-0-9931587-0-4 / 978-0-9931587-1-1

Message from Captivity

When diplomat's daughter Sophie Langley is sent to St Nicolas to care for her two elderly aunts, she finds herself trapped following the German invasion. In the Battle for France, linguist and poet Robert Anderson gets embroiled in an impossible military situation. From the beautiful Channel Islands to the very heart of Nazi-occupied Europe, *Message From Captivity* weaves factual authenticity into the fabric of a narrative where the twists and turns of captivity, freedom and dangerous pursuit have unforeseen consequences.

ISBN: 978-0-9931587-5-9 Also available on Kindle

The Girl in Jack's Portrait

A struggling barrister, a soldier, a divorcee, an architect, a businessman, a mental health nurse... Six people seeking an escape from their pasts and redemption in the present; six people who find their lives interwoven and their secrets revealed. But just who is the Girl in Jack's Portrait?

ISBN: 978-0-9931587-6-6 Also available on Kindle

Other publications by Ōzaru Books

Curling Wisps & Whispers of History

LucyAnn Curling

Vol. 1: Thanet to Tasmania

If family history is about gathering as many ancestors as possible, this book fails: it focuses on just three generations of the author's paternal side, between 1780 and 1826. At first nothing stirs the still waters of centuries of East Kent farming tradition. Men organize parish affairs, women follow domestic routines, boys attend a boarding school in Ramsgate, and only grandma seems interested in socializing or travel. Why then did Thomas Oakley Curling uproot everything and take his family on a marathon five-month voyage to Van Diemen's Land? Why leave one child behind? And where does Sir Charles Napier fit in?

The genealogical quest starts naturally with a family heirloom, but soon tangential questions emerge, as multiple threads are collated and woven into one story. 'Georgian & Regency ancestors' might sound remote, removed from our reality, but the individuals' letters draw us into their world, and copious illustrations punctuate the text, animating the environments in which they lived.

ISBN 978-1-915174-02-4

Vol. 2: Kent to Kefalonia

This second volume finds the Curling family back in England, struggling to find a financial foothold in society. Second son, Edward, has an unrewarding job in an attorney's office when Charles James Napier offers him a golden opportunity on the island of Kefalonia.

Follow the surprising twists of providence as Edward works on Napier's unusual project. What is the Malta connection? Tensions between Napier and his line manager, Sir Frederick Adam, have repercussions for Edward. Greece at this time was fighting for independence from the Ottoman Empire, and that war touches Napier's personal life obliquely but with lasting effect, while Edward's too is permanently changed by a different encounter. Edward's work journal and numerous letters in the Napier Papers at the British and Bodleian Libraries bear witness to the social pressures acting on all members of this extended clan, as their feelings come into conflict with accepted norms, and set the stage for further dramatic developments...

ISBN 978-1-915174-07-9

Other publications by Ōzaru Books

Reflections in an Oval Mirror

Memories of East Prussia, 1923-45

Anneli Jones

8 May 1945 – VE Day – was Anneliese Wiemer's twenty-second birthday. Although she did not know it then, it marked the end of her flight to the West, and the start of a new life in England. These illustrated memoirs, based on a diary kept during the Third Reich and letters rediscovered many decades later, depict the momentous changes occurring in Europe against a backcloth of everyday farm life in East Prussia (now the north-western corner of Russia).

ISBN: 978-0-9559219-0-2 Also on Kindle, and in German

Carpe Diem

The Ongoing Journey of an East Prussian Exile

This sequel to "Reflections in an Oval Mirror" details Anneli's post-war life. The scene changes from life in Northern 'West Germany' as a refugee, reporter and military interpreter, to parties with the Russian Authorities in Berlin, boating in the Lake District with the original 'Swallows and Amazons', weekends with the Astors at Cliveden, then the beginnings of a new family in a small Kentish village. Finally, after the fall of the Iron Curtain, Anneli is able to revisit her first home once more.

ISBN: 978-0-9931587-3-5

Skating at the Edge of the Wood

Memories of East Prussia, 1931-1945… 1993

Marlene Yeo

In 1944, the thirteen-year-old East Prussian girl Marlene Wiemer embarked on a horrific trek to the West, to escape the advancing Red Army. Her cousin Jutta was left behind the Iron Curtain. This book contains dramatic depictions of Marlene's flight, recreated from her letters to Jutta during the last year of the war, and contrasted with joyful memories of the innocence that preceded them.

Nearly fifty years later, the advent of perestroika meant that Marlene and Jutta were finally able to revisit their childhood home, after a lifetime of growing up under diametrically opposed societies, and the book closes with a final chapter revealing what they find.

ISBN: 978-0-9931587-2-8 Also on Kindle, and in German

Other publications by Ōzaru Books

Courtly Feasts to Kremlin Banquets
A History of Celebration and Hospitality: Echoes of Russia's cuisine

Mikami Oksana Zakharova and Sergey Pushkaryov
Translated & adapted by Marina George

This is a book not only for lovers of food but also for those with an appetite for adventure and a thirst for the discovery of exciting gastronomic delights.

Russian history presents us with a rich tapestry of extravagant ceremony, characterized not only by the magnificent grandeur of individual courtly feasts but also by successive generations of nobility actively vying with each other to surpass the splendour created by their predecessors. Russian hospitality has always exuded a special vitality and sense of warm-hearted sociability. In Old Russia there was also a significant link between hospitality and the teachings of the Orthodox Church.

The political and social history of Russia has seen some very violent changes. The more shocking the political events of a country, the more brutal the cultural changes can be. At times, the differences between the past and the present are so extreme that one is faced with completely different worlds. Despite dramatic and often heart-breaking upheavals, we do surely have a duty to remember those distant roots that helped to nourish the present.

"*Modern society contemptuously dismisses and sneers at the former way of life and deliberately breaks any connection with the past, which would always have been held to be so dear at the time.*" These words of writer, historian and theatre critic Yevgeny Opochinin were published in 1909 before the full horror of the revolutionary upheaval. The relevance of such remarks is surely as valid now as then.

Throughout history, special events have been an important way of imparting tradition from one generation to another, and symbolic meanings can still be found, if one knows the stories from the past. One just has to know where to look.

ISBN: 978-0-9931587-8-0

www.ingramcontent.com/pod-product-compliance
Lightning Source LLC
Chambersburg PA
CBHW030809310726
48980CB00006B/434/J

* 9 7 8 0 9 5 5 9 2 1 9 4 0 *